P9-CSA-136

SEEKING HER

By Cora Carmack

SEEKING HER

A Finding It Novella

CORA CARMACK

WILLIAM MORROW IMPULSE
An Imprint of HarperCollins*Publishers*

This is a work of fiction. Names, characters, places, and incidents are products of the author's imagination or are used fictitiously and are not to be construed as real. Any resemblance to actual events, locales, organizations, or persons, living or dead, is entirely coincidental.

SEEKING HER. Copyright © 2014 by Cora Carmack. All rights reserved under International and Pan-American Copyright Conventions. By payment of the required fees, you have been granted the nonexclusive, nontransferable right to access and read the text of this e-book on screen. No part of this text may be reproduced, transmitted, decompiled, reverse-engineered, or stored in or introduced into any information storage and retrieval system, in any form or by any means, whether electronic or mechanical, now known or hereinafter invented, without the express written permission of HarperCollins e-books.

EPub Edition FEBRUARY 2014 ISBN: 9780062299291

Print Edition ISBN: 9780062299307

10 9 8 7 6 5 4 3

For my parents,
who taught me not just to dream,
but to dream big.
And for Patrick and Shelly,
for all of your help
that allows me to keep on dreaming.

ACKNOWLEDGMENTS

THEY SAY WRITING a book takes a village, and in part that's because writing a book is never just as simple as putting words on a paper. The stars have to align (and a lot of people have to help) to turn those words into a finished project.

First, I have to thank HarperCollins, in particular my editor, Amanda, and my publicist, Jessie, for being 100% behind me and my books. Thanks also to Molly and Pam and every person whose hand touches my work—from copyediting to cover art. I'm glad to have found such a terrific home.

Second, thanks to my agent, Suzie. I say it all the time—to family and colleagues and even the eighty-year-old man sitting next to me on a plane who asked me about writing—signing with you and New Leaf was the best decision I could have possibly made. Thanks for handling all my crazy.

A giant thank you to Kelly for being so invested and so awesome at what you do. You know I'm a control freak, and I have trouble handing things over to others, but I have never, not once, hesitated to trust your skills and opinions. You're that awesome.

Thank you to Patrick and Shelly for attempting to help bring order to my chaos and for being fantastic friends. Thank you, Lindsay, for always being there when I need to vent or text for hours in caps lock. Bethany, thanks for always badgering me to name characters after you (and for taking care of Kitty Katniss while I'm off at signings).

Thank you to my family. I'm a hot mess most of the time, and somehow you guys manage to hold the pieces of me together even when you're a thousand miles away.

And to my fantastic readers and all the amazing bloggers who have supported me—I could not do any of this without you. I will always do my best to make it up to you guys with more books and posts of cute boys with cats. Sarah, Johana, and Christine, I hope you like your cameo appearances. And to all the readers that I've met at signings this year, I cannot even begin to express the ways in which you all have touched me—to all the kick-ass girls in Miami; to Antonella in Houston; to Ria, that I see everywhere; to Vilma; who is awesome; to Jeanne, who I shared HP and margaritas with; to my tattoo ladies in Oklahoma—I could probably go on forever. I've met so many wonderful people in so many wonderful cities, and every time I am humbled and amazed at the support and love you show me and books in general. Love you all!

SEEKING HER

1

I'D SPENT BLISTERINGLY hot days in the desert, followed by achingly cold nights. I'd been shot, nearly blown up, and sprayed with shrapnel like it was water. Now I was a glorified babysitter.

The universe has a strange sense of humor.

The pretty blonde stood a dozen rows ahead of me on the airplane, her nearly identical picture burning a hole in my back pocket. She was trying to shove a large backpack, not unlike the pack I had in the Marines, into the overhead compartment, and I was getting a long look at her body while she did it. Her baggy cotton T-shirt rode up to show a slim tanned waist. I cast my eyes down, but then they got stuck on hips covered by short denim cutoffs that gave way to long, equally tan legs. I looked away.

For a second.

What the hell. I was getting paid to look after her. In my book, that counted as permission to look. Plus, if I was going to be following her around a continent, I needed to be able to recognize her at the slightest glance.

That was a good enough excuse as far as I was concerned.

Her clothes reminded me of something you could find at a garage sale, but somehow on her, they worked. She appeared effortlessly beautiful, radiant in that way that you can't help but take a second look. But knowing her father and the world she came from, I'm sure that look was both purposeful and pricey.

With some girlie magazine tucked under her arm and a drink from Starbucks, she took a seat, and I couldn't see her anymore.

I sighed, already antsy, and we weren't even in the air yet. My knees pushed uncomfortably up against the seat in front of me. The old man next to me had already taken the armrest, and I leaned on the remaining armrest tilting my head against the seat back.

I was bored, and boredom and I did not mix well. I needed action and adrenaline and excitement. But I knew I was likely to be stuck with stuffy museums and tourist traps and prissy little European cafés.

The info her dad had given me said she just graduated with a Bachelors of Fine Arts, so I'd expected her to choose Paris or London—some place known for its artistic side.

Maybe Kiev was artsy.

I knew as little about this city as I knew about her.

Kelsey Ann Summers.

Twenty-two years old.

Recent college graduate.

Traveling around Europe. Indefinitely.

Which meant I'd be following her *indefinitely*.

In the grand scheme of things, it was a pretty great gig. Certainly better than the landscaping job I'd had (and been fired from). Beat that shitty office job that I wasted two weeks on, too. Boring or not, I'd be on the road. For whatever reason, I couldn't stand staying in one place right now. My father had been the one to negotiate this "job." He was tired of helping me out, and I was damn tired of needing him.

So Sorority Girl Stalker it was. Put that shit on my résumé.

The money sure as hell didn't hurt either.

I'd keep watch while she did her girlie stuff. I'd scan for pickpockets and make sure she stayed safe; and I'd get to see some of the world not through the windshield of a Humvee for once.

Win-win.

I only met her dad once, to sign the contract and pick up the thin file with Kelsey's information and his contact numbers. The whole thing was like some weird Bond movie, only with far fewer explosions and government secrets.

Mr. Summers was surprised he'd never met me, seeing as how our families ran in the same circles. I didn't tell him that that was because I was the black sheep of the family. Then he would have found someone else to follow his daughter, probably worried that I'd corrupt his little angel.

Speaking of Mr. Summers . . . I fished out the phone he'd given me, and sent him a short text to let him know we'd both made it onto our connecting flight in New York and were about to take off. He didn't respond before the glaring flight attendant told me to turn off my phone. I turned on airplane mode, pretended like I pressed down the power button, and then laid it facedown in my lap.

A few hours into the flight, the cabin had grown dark and the man next to me had been trying unsuccessfully to find a comfortable way to sleep for what felt like ages. Maybe it was cruel, but I sort of hoped he would remain unsuccessful. Just looking at him you could *tell* he was one of those guys that would accidentally snuggle up against you in his sleep.

He also had *drooler* written all over him.

No thank you.

On the edge of sleep, I leaned as far away from my restless neighbor as I could manage, my elbow on the outside armrest and my head on my hand.

Something bumped my arm, jostling me out of my almost-sleep. I looked up to see a familiar face. Her eyes were heavy with sleep and her hair was mussed. I wondered briefly if this was what she looked like first thing in the morning, then her eyes swept up toward mine. Cursing myself for my slow reaction time, I pulled the baseball cap on my head down lower and turned away as she mumbled, "Sorry."

I didn't answer, pretending to fall back into sleep.

I made sure to keep my limbs out of the aisle and my

head down. A few minutes later, I recognized the strappy sandals on her feet as she shuffled back toward the front of the plane.

I glanced up, careful to keep my hat down. The old woman sitting next to her had taken advantage of Kelsey's absence to get something out of her bag, and was now struggling to return the bag to the overhead bin above her.

Normally, I would have stood up to help, but I couldn't risk drawing any more attention to myself. I was banking on the darkness of the plane and Kelsey's obvious sleepiness to negate our earlier interaction.

Instead, I watched as Kelsey took the bag from the woman and lifted it up above her head. Her shirt rode up again, and this time my eyes didn't hesitate to search out the smooth skin of her waist.

Damn. I needed to reel that in ASAP.

I leaned my elbows on my knees and pressed my forehead into my knuckles. This didn't bode well for my self-control on this trip. It had never exactly been my strong suit. The Marines had helped with that, but I still had my weak points.

And a pretty blonde was definitely one of them.

Lust made men do stupid things.

Okay, me. Lust made *me* do stupid things.

People tend to notice when you openly stare at them. That particular stupid thing could send me packing on the first flight back to Houston in no time.

My father had already threatened me with a job at his company if I didn't shape up and stick with something, and that was something I'd never had any desire to do. Sooner or later, I would run out of jobs willing to take a chance on someone with my track record, and I'd be forced to accept it. Then I'd be right back on the track that had sent me off the deep end nearly a decade ago. But this time, I wouldn't have the Marines to pull me out of it.

I turned up my music as loud as I could stand it and settled back in my seat, determined to get some sleep.

This was a job. Plain and simple. I *had* to think of it that way. And since it would be easy for the next ten hours or so, I should rest now while I could. The real job would begin when we landed in the Ukraine.

I closed my eyes, glad at least that the Marines had taught me how to sleep just about anywhere. This was a mission. Just like all the rest. And it was a hell of a lot easier than any of the others I'd had over the years.

IT DIDN'T TAKE long after landing for me to realize that this job wouldn't be nearly as easy as I had anticipated.

I'd thought it was kind of ridiculous when Mr. Summers gave me a phone with a GPS tracker linked to Kelsey's. I had assumed I'd just get up early, watch for her to leave, and then follow. She'd go back to her hotel. I'd wait for her to go to sleep, then snag some rest of my own.

Oh, how very wrong I'd been.

I checked into an inn across the street from her hostel in Kiev, specifically requesting a room that faced the street and would give me a good view of her coming and going.

I got my key and climbed the narrow stairs to the room, pulling my phone out of my pocket on the way. I dialed the number Kelsey's father had given me, and a woman answered.

"Mr. Summer's office."

I cleared my throat. "Yes, um, this is Jackson Hunt." I wasn't sure how much further to identify myself. Daughter Stalker wasn't exactly a title I was ready to throw around in public.

"Yes, Mr. Hunt. Mr. Summers is in a meeting, but he was expecting your call. You arrived safely?"

"Yes, we both did."

"Excellent. He'll be in touch."

The line went dead. I stood still in front of my door for a few moments.

That was somehow less . . . dramatic than I thought it would be. I was glad I wasn't the only one handling this matter-of-factly.

I fit the old-fashioned key into the lock and entered the room. I deposited my stuff on a simple bed with spindly legs and a thin mattress, then glanced out the window—just in time to glimpse Kelsey fleeing the hostel on the back of some guy's moped.

"Oh, fuck me."

I grabbed a few key items and powered up the app that linked me to her phone. Cursing, I took the stairs two at a time, as fast I could, down to the lobby. I ran out into the street, but she was long gone.

"*Goddamn it.*"

A tourist couple with fanny packs (yes, actual fanny packs) jumped in response to my swear.

Easy, Hunt. Blend in.

That's what this mission required. I needed to get good at it, and fast. My heart beat loudly in my ears as I waited for the app to finish loading. I was trained to operate under pressure. Panic should not have been a problem, but this was different.

First, it's a lot easier to fight a person than to protect one. And when I did protect someone, it was usually a guy in combat gear who had a gun of his own. And I knew those guys. I knew their tendencies, their strengths, and their weaknesses.

I was beginning to realize just how little I knew about Kelsey Summers.

The phone pinged, and I watched a moving blue dot that I guessed was her. She was already a couple miles away. I jogged down to a busier corner and flagged down a taxi. It wasn't until I slid across the cracked leather seat that I realized I couldn't tell him where I was going because I had no fucking clue.

His dark eyes met mine expectantly through the rearview mirror, and I held up a finger to buy some time. I'd bought a Ukrainian phrasebook in the airport on a whim while Kelsey was in the bathroom. I felt a trickle of sweat run down the back of my neck as I dug it out of my bag and flipped through the first few pages frantically.

One look at the letters that I didn't recognize (or have

any idea how to pronounce), and I knew the phrasebook was going to do jack shit for me.

"English?" I asked the driver.

He didn't need to reply. I got the giant, resounding no just from the slant of his thick eyebrows.

I tried showing him the app, hoping maybe he would recognize the interface of a GPS or be able to recognize what part of the city that blue dot was currently moving through, but his eyebrows only furrowed further.

Defeated, I smiled, threw him a couple coins for his trouble, and then climbed out of the cab, now even farther away from Kelsey and with no idea how I was going to get to her.

It took me exactly ten minutes to figure out that my Ukrainian phrasebook was largely useless (not just because I was useless when it came to using it, but because most of the people I ran across spoke Russian instead).

Did Kelsey speak Russian? I may not have gone to college, but I didn't think the average rich girl from Texas would be fluent in the language. Then again, given the chance to go to Europe, the average girl would have probably chosen London or Paris or Rome.

Maybe she knew that guy on the moped. Except, her father didn't mention anything about Kelsey visiting friends (or a boyfriend) overseas. But then again, he ran in the same circles as my father, who made it a point to be as oblivious as possible, so perhaps he just didn't know.

Or maybe that boyfriend was why he sent me. Maybe he was dangerous.

Frustrated, I rubbed my hand across the top of my shorn head, not for the first time, missing the longer hair I'd had before enlisting. You'd think after two tours, I would be used to it, but I wasn't. Groaning, I decided that I wasn't getting any closer to her by standing around. And the idea of her being God-knows-where with that guy had my insides clenching uncomfortably.

I set off on foot, too annoyed and worried to actually look around me at the city. I could only stare at that dot and know that I was fucking this up as badly as everything else in my life.

Finally, after another ten minutes, the dot stopped moving. I walked for a little longer, and when I was certain that Kelsey wasn't going to take off again, I worked on finding someone who could help me figure out where she was and how to get there.

There was a moment when I assumed the worst about her unmoving dot. Maybe it was because I'd lived amidst war for more than a fourth of my life. But I shook that off. The Ukraine wasn't war torn, not right now anyway. She was probably sitting down in a café or on a park bench.

My deliverance came in the form of a cute little girl with scuffed shoes, curly hair, and a gap-toothed smile. She couldn't have been more than seven or eight, but she understood me. My words anyway. She directed her big brown doe eyes at my phone, but she was a little too young to help me figure out how the map translated to the city of Kiev.

"Ivan!" she called out. Her tiny fingers circled around her mouth, pressing into her chubby cheeks, and she yelled louder, "Ivan! Идите сюда!"

An older boy, distinctly preteen with messy hair and pimples, came bounding over toward us.

"Что?" he said, annoyed.

Her tiny lips moved faster, words with too many consonants pouring from her mouth, as her hands took up residence on her hips.

Ivan, who I guessed was her brother, rolled his eyes and held out his hand toward me.

I handed over my phone, then watched as he studied it with a bit more comprehension than his sister. He turned it sideways, then back again.

"Botanical gardens," he said. "Near the monastery."

"Can I take a cab there? If I say 'botanical gardens' will they know what I mean?"

Ivan rubbed at a pimple on his chin, and then shrugged. "Metro is easier." He pointed down the street and said, "There. To universytet."

"University?"

"Yes. Is next to botanical gardens."

I nodded. "Okay. Okay, thank you, Ivan." I knelt down in front of the little girl, and I noticed the bottom of her dress was smudged with dirt. "And thank you, too."

"Sasha," Ivan told me.

"You were very helpful, Sasha."

Her grin was adorable.

Sometimes, I wondered if I might have turned out differently if I'd had siblings. If I'd had a little sister like her to look after and protect, maybe I wouldn't have gotten lost so deeply in my own troubles.

But there was no time to think of that now, to wander through the minefields of my past, not when I had someone who needed me in the present.

2

I EMERGED FROM the metro right next to the university, and the botanical gardens were easy enough to spot. They were situated right next to a monastery. Green domed roofs and golden spires took up the forefront of my view while the gardens stretched out behind it. With a river at my back and the cool breeze carrying the scent of flowers, I was distracted for a moment from my search.

If I didn't need to find her, this would be the perfect place to draw.

Sketching calmed me. Maybe because it brought order to a disordered world. But it more than that. It allowed me to do more than just fix a chaotic world; it let me escape it. By focusing on the page, I forgot about everything around me. I stepped onto another plane and found peace in something beautiful. And though sometimes this seemed impossible in all the world's ugliness, there was always at least one beautiful thing.

At the moment there was much more than one.

The smell of the gardens was unlike anything I'd ever experienced, light and sweet and seductive all at the same time. The breeze teased through the canopy of trees, and it hit me then how tired the flight halfway around the world had left me.

I blinked, shook my head, and stretched my neck.

Focus, Hunt. This is not a vacation for you.

I referenced the GPS on my phone again. The garden was full of winding trails, and there wasn't a straight line between Kelsey and me, not without trekking through some, no doubt, rare and expensive greenery.

So I guessed as best I could. Whenever there was a chance to turn in Kelsey's direction, I took that path. Sometimes it would wind in a completely different direction, and I'd have to double back and try a different trail. I should have picked up some kind of map or something, but I didn't.

So phone in hand, I did my best.

Finally, I was close enough that she should be just around the bend.

Only the trail I was on didn't curve; it remained straight and steady right past where the app said Kelsey should be.

I stopped, puzzled.

Maybe a different trail would circle around to where she was.

I trekked back to the last path I'd been on and took the next turn toward Kelsey, sure that that path would lead me to her.

It didn't.

Once again, I found the trail I walked curving away from where my phone said my target was.

Sighing, I cast my eyes around to make sure there was no

one else around, and then stepped off the path and into a wooded area that I hoped wasn't off limits. Twigs crunched beneath my boots, and even though I was doing something that could potentially get me kicked out, I felt at ease.

I'd always been more at home in the wilderness. You'd think growing up in Texas that I would have had my fill of it, but not in my family. Golfing was about as close to nature as my father got.

I shrugged off my thoughts and worries and sank into the sounds of nature. I focused on the GPS and enjoyed the steady rhythm of my steps through the woods.

I slowed when I neared the area where Kelsey was supposed to be, so that I didn't give myself away. Stepping carefully, I moved quietly between the trees. I kept expecting to peek around a trunk and see her, but she wasn't there.

Not even when I was right on top of the signal.

That's when I saw her backpack, tossed into the dirt beside a bush, a water bottle, some lipstick, and a passport spilling out of its open top.

My heart thudded once, and then picked up, double time.

Adrenaline sharpened my vision. Careful to keep an eye on my surroundings, I stole past my hiding spot and knelt beside the backpack. I flipped open the passport, and there she was. God, even her passport picture was gorgeous. Long tousled blond hair and vivid green eyes.

I closed the little book, squeezing it between my fingers, then scanned my surroundings again.

Maybe my original inclination to panic hadn't been so far off.

I made myself slow down and consider the facts.

She'd not made any phone calls upon arrival, unless she'd made them in the restroom at the airport. That was the only time she was out of my sight. I'd followed her on the metro and through the streets to her hostel. I'd watched her check in, and everything had seemed normal.

Assuming she would take a little bit to get settled, I'd snuck off around the corner to the inn we'd passed by on the way to her hostel.

I tried to recall her and the guy she'd gone off with on the moped.

Her cheek had rested against his back, so he was taller. She was fairly tall herself, so I guessed that would put him at maybe six foot three. My height, or close to it. He'd worn a helmet, so I had no idea what he looked like, only that he was bigger, enough to overpower her, if that's what he wanted.

Her hands had gripped his jacket, not his waist. What did that mean? If he were a boyfriend, surely she would have held on to him instead of his clothes.

Something in me relaxed at that notion, but at the same time more anxiety flooded my already aching head.

If he wasn't a boyfriend, that meant she'd gone off with a complete stranger. But why?

Just when I was about to give up hope of my stealthy role and start yelling her name, I heard laughter behind me.

I edged around the bush, and saw two legs stretching out behind a tree. Dark jeans and boots, not the short-shorts and strappy shoes that Kelsey had been wearing.

I retreated back behind another line of trees, and then carefully maneuvered my way closer.

A white shirt hung, snagged on a branch, swaying in the floral breeze. That should have given me a clue. But my mind was still in mission mode, so I continued my slow, silent steps until I saw Kelsey—shirtless . . . straddling who I guessed was her moped driver.

I mouthed a curse word, but I didn't look away.

Her skin was smooth and tan, and I was fascinated by the trail of her spine, the way it deepened like an empty riverbed when she arched forward. The tips of her hair danced across her back, swaying with her movements. Her bra was emerald green, almost like her eyes; and my mouth went dry when she leaned back—and I got a full view of her. I could almost ignore the guy who was with her and the way he trailed kisses down her neck to her collarbone. I could almost pretend that this wasn't a billion different kinds of wrong.

Almost.

I was stuck, frozen in place, helpless to do anything but stare at her, at the complete abandon written across her face.

Who knows how long I would have stayed there if the guy hadn't looked up and met my eyes.

I mouthed a few four-letter words and spun away, pressing my back against the tree.

He said something, and I got ready to run.

"What?" Kelsey asked, her voice so breathy and sensuous that it brought the image of her back into my mind with such perfection that I would have believed I was seeing it for real.

Damn it. This is a mission. Focus.

The guy repeated himself, louder this time, in another language.

"That sounds gorgeous, but I don't know what you're saying."

Slow and unsure, the guy said, "Man."

"Yes, that's you," Kelsey replied with a laugh.

"No. Man."

Behind me, there was shuffling, and I heard Kelsey scoff, "Hey."

I noted that as my cue to leave, and I took off, careful to dart behind trees until I was far enough away that I could make an all-out run for it. I didn't stop when I hit the trail, but kept on going until I was back to the more populated areas of the garden, where I could blend in around other people. I found a spot on the steps and picked up a newspaper when someone else abandoned it. I couldn't read the printed words, but I welcomed the sanctuary as I hid behind the thin sheets of paper.

Fucking hell, that was messed up.

My job for the foreseeable future was protecting a girl who followed a complete stranger (who barely even spoke her language) into the woods to hook up. It was so fucking careless, and I was beginning to understand exactly why her father had gone to such lengths to make sure she was taken care of during this trip.

Jesus. And I had thought this would be *boring*.

Goddamn stressful was more like it.

As annoyed as I was with her, I was infinitely more annoyed with myself. I was the dumbass who almost got caught because I couldn't pull my eyes away from her.

I had to get that shit under control or she would make me in no time. And I needed to take this seriously. This guy hadn't hurt her, but I knew firsthand that there were plenty of people out in the world willing to take advantage of her particular brand of naïveté.

I kept my phone perched on my knee, watching that sedentary blue dot out of the corner of my eye. It was another fifteen minutes or so before it began to move. Five more before I saw Kelsey and her foreign friend emerge from the dirt trail onto the paved steps at the center of the garden.

They passed by me and I scowled, expecting the two of them to go back to wherever his moped was parked, leaving me to chase behind again.

I was surprised when Kelsey stopped at the bottom of the steps and said something to him. He paused and leaned his ear closer to her mouth like that might help him understand her better. She took a few steps back and gestured toward the garden. He looked confused, but her intentions became pretty clear when she started climbing the steps and waved goodbye.

He stared after her for a few moments, his mouth open

and his brows furrowed. His eyes dropped to her legs, and he grinned in a way that was both sorrowful and celebratory at the same time. Sad to see her go, but victorious all the same.

He ran his fingers through his mussed hair, and then turned back in the direction he'd been heading. I had a feeling that we wouldn't be seeing him again, and felt stupid for being glad.

I turned sideways so that I could see where Kelsey was heading. I waited until she'd left the steps of the courtyard and turned down one of the paths. I got up and followed her, tucking the newspaper in my back pocket in case I needed it again for cover.

I followed at a distance, but the stealth wasn't really necessary. She didn't stop to smell any flowers or pause to take a picture. She walked quickly, determinedly forward like there was somewhere specific she meant to go.

Still, I held back, wanting to be cautious after nearly getting caught before. I was glad I did when, several minutes later, I started to round a bend only to find her stopped and scanning the area around her. I stepped off the path and into a thatch of trees where she couldn't see me.

When she was satisfied that she was alone, she dropped her backpack beside the trail and walked up to an old, very large tree. The branches were thick and numerous; she gravitated toward a limb that dipped low to the ground, the spears of grass skimming its bark.

She tested its strength with her hand and then, satisfied, sat down on it. She wrapped her arms around herself, grasping both elbows, and laid back along the limb.

I might have thought she was sunbathing, except she took no care to lie in a place with direct sunlight, nor did she uncross her arms.

I thought maybe she was resting, taking a nap even, except I could see the steady, constant tap of her sandal from here.

I wanted to move closer, to see her face and try to decipher what was going through her head. Had she been heading for this particular tree? Or was she just looking for solitude? I brushed away a niggling of guilt at intruding.

I was reading things into her posture, into the rhythm of her tapping foot, and I couldn't tell whether she was truly upset or if I just wanted her to be.

For all I knew, she was as relaxed as could be.

There was nothing that said women couldn't have meaningless sex. I'd had my fair share, and it was only double-standard assholes that didn't seem to think that that was okay.

And I didn't want to be that guy.

But I couldn't shake the feeling that whatever Kelsey was feeling, relaxed wasn't it.

I resisted the urge to move closer. The trail was wide open next to her. There was no sneaking up on her now, not like when she'd been in the woods.

So I had to wait, with just conjecture and my GPS for company. If only that little app could tell me where her mind was along with her body.

Not that *that* mattered. How she was feeling had nothing to do with my job. I just needed to keep her safe. But then again . . . how she was feeling would influence her actions, which did matter to me.

When the sun's light was low in the sky, casting angled shadows across the trail, Kelsey sat up.

I strained my eyes to see if she'd been crying or if there was any other signal of meaning for her little break.

I got nothing.

She looked as perfect as ever, and I decided that it had all been me, seeing what I wanted to see. She was fine.

I made a promise to myself once and for all to turn off the emotional side of this. I needed to be as objective as possible if this was going to work.

From now on, I would watch her when I could.

Find her when I'd lost her.

Protect her when she needed me.

That was it. Nothing else.

3

TEMPTATION. IF THIS mission had a code name, that would be it.

Not just Kelsey, though the girl was temptation at it's finest, but everything about it. It was hard to stay focused on work when "the office" was a bar.

I'd pretty much decided that she was a spoiled rich girl, and that made her easier to resist. But having daddy's credit card meant she had no shortage of outfits designed just to bring men to their knees.

She was wearing one now— a short white lacy skirt that made her tan skin seem to glow in the light of the bar. Her shirt hung off one shoulder in a way that was supposed to look like an accidental peek of skin, but definitely wasn't. And there was just something about the plateau of her shoulder that made you want to lay your lips against it for a taste.

That wasn't the only thing beckoning for a taste, though.

I watched her lick her lips before tipping back some dark concoction in a shot glass that tonight's guy had bought for her.

I clenched my fists harder, wincing at the stinging cuts my short nails made into my palm, and focused my eyes elsewhere. I wasn't here to have a good time. I busied myself scanning the bar for potential hazards.

The only potential danger I saw was a drunk guy weaving through the tables. And he was mostly in danger of knocking over any drink within a ten-foot radius.

I redirected my gaze to Kelsey in time to see her finish a shot and then take a lime from between some dude's lips.

A few seconds later, she grinned wildly, like she was having the best fucking time of her life.

I envied her that.

I'd certainly done my fair share of partying. I could still remember the first party I'd attended in high school. I'd been a freshman, and when I made varsity basketball, the team invited me out with them.

My first shot of tequila had burned like rubbing alcohol, and I ended that night blowing chunks into the pool in the backyard.

Funny how something so terrible could be nostalgic now.

Maybe Kelsey's dad was strict. The fact that he hired me certainly meant that he was controlling. Maybe she was just sowing her wild oats. And as much as I didn't want to be here, I couldn't exactly begrudge her the chance to loosen up.

And damn, was she good at loosening up.

The music was electronic and kind of all over the place. It made it even harder to focus on the task at hand, and I could feel the beginning of a headache pulsing above my eyebrow.

I heard a shrill shriek on the other side of the bar and jumped to attention. My mind ordered my feet to move, and I got a few steps before I really catalogued the situation.

Kelsey wasn't in trouble.

Not really.

A guy with dark hair and model good-looks had lifted her up to sit on the bar, and she was laughing as he pushed her to stand up on it.

She shook her head, her smile so wide that it shone in the dim bar. The guy said something, his fingers pressing into her waist. She laughed, throwing her head back. Her hair fanned out behind her, and my fingers itched to freeze time and sketch her in that moment.

Her eyes closed—she looked transported. Like she lived on some other plane, one brighter and more beautiful than ours. And I wasn't the only one who thought so. Eyes all across the bar were pinned on her, no doubt drawn by the same inexplicable essence that made me unable to take my eyes off of her, regardless of what I was *supposed* to be doing. In that moment, I think *everyone* envied her.

And if she was magnetic then, she was downright hypnotic when she pulled up her feet, and balanced her hands against her date to stand up on the bar.

A group had formed around her, people that she'd spent the night flitting between like the ultimate social butterfly. They laughed and cheered, drawn to her like moths to the flame. And maybe I was too, because before I realized it, I was less than a dozen feet away, leaning against the bar.

She swayed her hips, and the electronic music that had seemed chaotic before made sense when seen through the movement of her body. The music was . . . restless, a description that worked when applied to Kelsey, too.

Despite being the center of this entire bar's attention, her eyes were flicking around, constantly on the lookout for what was next, waiting for something more. I couldn't tell if it was boredom that had her always looking ahead or something else.

She bent, giving me (and everyone else) a long look at her legs. When she stood, she'd pulled another girl up on top of the bar with her. Within minutes, the bartender had cranked up the music and the vibe of the entire bar changed.

Where before all the chairs had been filled, now it was the aisles and the open space that were overflowing. People were dancing on their own, in pairs, and in groups. But still . . . every few seconds they seemed to cast their eyes up to the girl dancing on the bar, the girl who had single-handedly turned the night upside down.

I sat down on a stool, watching her, too. It was impossible not to. A few other girls had joined her on the bar, and Kelsey seemed completely oblivious to all the guys who were practically salivating below.

I was *far* from oblivious.

A song came on, some remixed version of an American hit that I couldn't stand, and she threw her arms up and declared to no one, "I love this song."

She sang the words at the top of her lungs, bouncing around in a way that made her look younger, less concerned with being pretty or sexy. I found myself smiling in spite of myself.

The bartender came over, completely nonplussed by the change in atmosphere. He leaned across the bar, and lifted his chin in acknowledgment.

"Я могу вам помочь?"

I paused, not just because I didn't speak the language. It was obvious what he was asking, and I hesitated.

I hadn't meant to come near the bar. That was the promise I made myself as soon as I followed Kelsey into the dimly lit building.

I swallowed, and my throat felt as dry as sandpaper. I was suddenly so *thirsty*.

"No." I shook my head vehemently. "No thank you."

I pushed my stool back and made for my original perch on the far wall. It was safer over there.

But the easiness I'd felt watching her was gone. By the time she quit the bar that night, her arm tucked into the elbow of the good-looking guy who'd lifted her up onto the bar, I'd worn my palms raw from clenching my fists.

I breathed a heady sigh of relief when I stepped out into the night air.

Mission Temptation was off to a rocky start.

IT WAS EASY that first night to think that Kelsey was just having a good time, enjoying her freedom. On the second night, I chalked it up to celebrating being in a new country.

But on the third day, when she ventured out to a club once again, I felt myself growing weary. She didn't do much during the day, slept late after her busy night. I couldn't seem to get myself to follow her lead. So I woke up at a reasonable time, texted her father to let him know where we were and that everything was fine, and tried my best to establish a routine.

She'd venture out for dinner (which was really lunch for her), then she'd repeat the whole adventure at a new venue.

Tonight, my control was wearing thin. We were at some dance club, and I kept losing sight of her on the dance floor. The first few times, I let it slide, searching until I found her again. Then I lost sight of her for nearly fifteen minutes, and knew that my current tactic wasn't working. I couldn't do shit to protect her if something happened while I was out on the edges of the dance floor.

I gritted my teeth, my annoyance simmering beneath my skin, and pushed through the crowds on the dance floor, heading in the direction where I'd last seen Kelsey.

I didn't make it very far before a drunk girl stumbled into me, spilling her nearly full drink down the front of my body.

I winced at the cold splash of liquid, and sucked in a breath. She started apologizing, but that mostly consisted of her touching me and then trying to goad me into dancing with her. I held her at arm's length, my jaw clenched so tight that I was probably grinding my teeth to dust.

I managed to extricate myself from her, only to turn and come face-to-face with a scantily clad girl making the rounds with a tray of colorful concoctions in plastic test tubes. I'd seen Kelsey down a few of them earlier, and the waitress held one up to me in offering.

My hand was reaching for it before my mind could do anything about it. Seconds before the tube was in my hand, I came to my senses. I pulled away from her so fast that I bumped into the drunk girl again, who spilled even more alcohol on my clothes.

Struggling to keep my breathing steady, I pushed my way a little too forcefully out of the crowd and back toward the edge of the room. I commandeered the first empty chair I found, slamming myself down into it and burying my head in my hands.

One year.

Well, almost.

I was *almost* one-year sober.

Less than two weeks until I would hit that milestone. If I were back home, I'd be getting my one-year chip, and I couldn't help but wonder if this would be any easier if I had it now to squeeze in my fist.

But I didn't have that chip. And I hadn't yet made it

to one year. Sweat was beading on my fucking forehead just from the determination it took to keep myself in the chair instead of searching out a drink. The smell of whiskey wafting up from my drenched shirt sure as hell wasn't helping.

I pressed my knuckles into my forehead hard, and then sat back, staring up at the ceiling. I watched the moving lights that flashed neon colors around the room and tried to clear my head.

Alcohol had been my crutch for a long time. It had practically raised me when my parents weren't around to do the job. Stepping away from my dysfunctional liquid family hadn't been easy. It had taken a war, a new family, and daily reminders of the thin line between life and death for me to beat it.

Here, I was alone, and exposed in a way that I hadn't allowed myself to be in a long time.

"Damn it," I groaned under my breath.

I could do this. I just needed to redirect all this energy into something else. Something active was usually best.

My eyes found Kelsey again on the dance floor. Unbidden, the thought rose that she would make an ideal distraction.

Immediately, I shut that down.

I was *not* trading one bad decision for another. Besides, she was the one who'd gotten me in this mess to start with. If alcohol sent me off the rails, then Kelsey was likely to send me off a cliff.

I just . . . I needed to get out of here.

Yes, I was supposed to protect her and that didn't include leaving her in this massive crowd. But I wouldn't be any help to her if I caved and had a drink.

The best thing for both of us right now was for me to get some distance.

4

HALFWAY BACK TO the inn, I realized I was practically stomping my way home. My teeth had been clenched so tight that my entire head ached. I was pissed. Pissed that I was even in this situation, that Kelsey wasn't who I'd expected her to be.

Sure, I hadn't relished the idea of following her to museums or plays or whatever, but that would have been better than this. Better than risking my precariously balanced life so she could party it up like a high school kid.

God, I was a fucking killjoy without alcohol. What I wouldn't give to be as carefree as Kelsey. Angry seemed to by my primary emotion these days. How had Rodriguez and the other guys put up with me?

A misplaced smile cracked across my lips. They hadn't, that's how. They'd never had any problem telling me when I was being a pain in the ass.

My skin flashed hot and then cold with the memory of my old unit. Still much more bitter than sweet.

There was a military ban on alcohol for much of the time I'd spent in Afghanistan, but it happened anyway. I kept clear of it for the most part, but one night, I'm not even sure how, I ended up with a bottle in my hand. Rodriguez found me, took it away, and then used it for firing practice.

He told me that I had the unfortunate problem of fighting two wars at once, and I'd find myself losing them both if I wasn't careful.

I wished he were here to talk me down now.

But he wasn't.

And that was another war within me, too.

I settled for stepping into the shower in my room, still fully clothed. I let the water weigh down the fabric, hopefully removing all traces of the alcohol that had been spilled on me. When I was satisfied, I shucked the heavy material and hung my clothes up on a hand rail on the tiled wall. Then I stood under the steaming water and tried to wash away the thoughts too. I closed my eyes and let the water pour over my face.

I was going to have to find some way to cope with this. If not, I was better off calling Mr. Summers and suggesting he find someone else to take over his daughter-watch.

I felt a pang of something at that thought. It was a general kind of discomfort, and I wasn't sure whether it was the thought of returning home or something else that made that thought so unappealing.

After the cooling walk earlier, and now standing under the calming rush of water, it was easier to think that I could control myself, but I knew better. It always seemed easier in my head than it really was.

I wiped the water from my eyes, and tried to think of some other way to deal. There was always the hope that Kelsey would get bored. That she would mellow out. If she only partied a couple nights a week, I should be able to resist. But that seemed unlikely.

All that restless energy; the way she'd soaked up the attention from the people around her. I couldn't see her giving that up. And it was working for her. She was still in the phase where partying made her feel good. That was the one thing that helped me stay clean. The few times I'd slipped up since I started the program had left me miserable and angry, and even more frustrated than when I started. I'd found new ways to chase the high. And maybe that wasn't any healthier, not when one way involved being in the midst of flying bullets.

It wasn't the same kind of rush, but it did the trick. I pictured Kelsey again, laughing with her head thrown back, her shirt falling off her shoulder and displaying the gentle curve of her neck. It reminded me of the way she'd tossed her head back that first day out in the woods.

The memory of that caused a different kind of rush in me, and I groaned, pressing my forehead into the tile. Before I could help myself, I pictured her long legs straddling that guy in the gardens. The bright green material of her bra, and the way it conformed to her perfect chest. She leaned back, her fingertips trailing from the bark of the tree to his shoulders.

In an instant, the memory shifted into fantasy, and those were my shoulders she clung to, not his.

That was my undoing. There was only so much resisting I could do in one night. Letting go of any thoughts about what was right or appropriate, I imagined what it would be like to have her legs clamped down around my hips, and her fingernails digging into my skin. I imagined her long hair tickling my arms as I smoothed my hands down her back to those maddeningly short shorts.

I closed my eyes to shut out the world, and let my hand drift down to one problem that was all too easy to solve.

I thought about her lips, red and full and taunting. I dreamed about the taste of her and the warmth of her skin. Remembering the way everyone flocked to her in that bar, the way she seemed to light a fire under the world, just the thought of having her all to myself—all this was enough to make my breath come in pants.

I didn't even have to invent anything more to get off. The memories alone did the trick, and my release was powerful enough to make my legs go weak and black spots merge in my vision. I didn't realize until afterward that the water sliding down my back had turned cold. Almost as if the universe were trying to keep me from crossing that line.

Too late.

MY EYES FOUND Kelsey, her hips once again swinging to the music. Bodies swarmed around her in the club and lights flashed overhead. There was a crash like thunder, and the club floor shook. Kelsey kept on dancing, oblivious, but I looked down to the rifle in my hands.

The rest of the world came into focus—the helmet strapped tight beneath my chin, the vest heavy against my chest, and the smoke singeing my nostrils.

Sand began to roll across my boots, riding on the wind and stinging the few places where my bare skin showed. In seconds, the club became a desert and the colored lights morphed into the flare of explosions. I was knocked off my feet, my ears ringing, but my eyes went to Kelsey once more, still standing. I heard the tap-tap-tap of gunfire, almost benign in it's simplicity. If we were somewhere else, it could have blended in with the sound of street traffic or construction. But in the desert, the sand seemed to suck away all the other sounds.

Tap-tap-tap.

I stood, whirling, trying to find the source, and I wasn't alone. Rodriguez was there at my heels. Ingram, Johnny One, and Teague, too.

"Come on!" Ingram roared, gesturing for us to retreat back behind a barricade. He slid over the top, knocking down glasses and beer bottles perched along the bar.

I looked back to Kelsey. She was alone on the dance floor now, the others running for cover, but still she danced. A blast struck off to my left, closer this time, and the ground rumbled so long it could have been an earthquake. I glanced back again, and everyone was behind the barricade, except for Rodriguez. I couldn't hear him over the near constant tap-tap-tap filling up the desert, but he was waving wildly.

I had to get Kelsey first. She was my responsibility.

I sprinted toward her, my boots sinking into the sand. A cloud of the stuff swirled up around us when I slid to a stop in front of her. My hands scrabbled at her hips, trying to take hold. Her long eyelashes rested against her cheeks, and it took a few seconds before her lids lifted. Her green eyes glowed, magnified by her spreading smile. I was stunned into stillness for a moment.

Tap-tap-tap-tap.

I heard the whine of a bullet ripping past on the wind, and I pulled Kelsey under my arm, ready to drag her with me.

I turned to see Rodriguez halfway toward me, his rifle hanging at his side. Tap-tap.

The bullets reached him before we heard the sound, so that his body seemed to jerk in anticipation. I didn't see where the first bullet hit, but the second struck in the neck. Blood painted the sand, and Rodriguez reached one hand out to me and the other toward his neck. The strap of his gun fell down to his elbow, and the weight must have been too much for him to reach his neck. He plunged toward me, his mouth hanging open as he tried and failed to draw in a breath. He sputtered around drifts of blood, and his eyes screamed at me in a way he couldn't.

I too felt like I was choking on the blood as his knees hit the earth, sand clumping into dark red clots beneath him. Kelsey's jaw dropped beside me in a scream, but I couldn't hear her. Silence rang in my ears like the first few seconds after a blast, but it stretched on. And despite being unable to hear, I knew the gasping, gurgling sound that Rodriguez's trembling mouth made like it was a physical thing I could see and touch.

It was Kelsey that began dragging me away, past the lifeless body of my friend. When I ripped my eyes off of him, I saw everything clearer. Including my friends behind the barricade, behind the bar.

My mind tripped for a moment, trying to reconcile the past and the present. The film of the dream weakened and I thought—I'm about to wake up. Relief pumped through my veins seconds before the mortar shell dropped and the bar exploded, flames propelled upward into the sky.

The blast blew me backward, and I was skidding through the sand. The last thing I saw before blacking out was Rodriguez's empty eyes and blood-stained lips.

I woke, covered in sweat as if I'd just spent the night in the desert heat. My ears rang as I stumbled out of bed and pushed open the window. Head swimming, I thought I might be sick. I concentrated on the purple pre-dawn sky.

The window shutters banged against the building in an eerily familiar tap-tap-tap, and I slid down to my knees. Turning, I sat with my back below the windowsill and tried to catch my breath.

I couldn't decide what was worse. Dreams like the one I'd just had, amalgamations of truth and fiction, or the ones that were actual memories. Rodriguez's death in my dream wasn't entirely unfamiliar. It bore a resemblance to the death of a soldier from the first week of my deployment. I couldn't remember that soldier's name now. —There had been too many others that I'd met and lost since then—but the look on his face . . . . that was still burned into my memory.

I reached for my backpack, fumbling with the zipper. Cursing my shaky fingers, I practically ripped the thing open. Just touching my sketchbook calmed me. I skimmed my finger up the metal spiral on the side and took a deep breath.

I flipped it open and came face-to-face with a blank page, a fresh start.

I closed my eyes, searching for something that could distract me. I decided on the ultimate distraction.

Kelsey.

I wasn't sure how I felt about her. My thoughts were a mess of frustration and want and annoyance. If I wasn't following her into bars, I wouldn't be so wound up. The dreams only happened when I was stressed. But I couldn't seem to pluck up much anger at her, not after last night when I'd allowed myself to think of her in an entirely different manner.

She was spoiled and reckless and shallow, and yet . . . there was something else to her. Something that I saw but couldn't put a name to. I thought back to the moments that I'd watched her that had felt the most honest. I thought of her dancing on that bar, carefree and unaware of her surroundings. She'd been almost childlike. Then there was that day in the park, her solitary hour in that tree, thinking about God knows what. I wanted to know where she went during those moments, because she wasn't in the present. She was like an old movie, where the film would catch or skip, ruining the illusion. I wanted to grab hold of that inconsistency, unravel it, and see the real story underneath.

More than that, I wanted to *capture* it. My fingers were itching to draw her.

So, I did.

I started with her neck, the way it had been tilted backward when she sat on the bar. I did a rough outline of her body—the bend of her knees, the point of her toes, the flare of her hips. I scratched out the swoop of her shirt as it hung off her shoulder.

It was a fairly accurate depiction, I thought, considering I was drawing from memory. But an hour in, I'd worn out my eraser trying to get her face right.

I knew what it looked like. Full lips, oval face, thin nose, expressive eyes. I had the pieces right. I was sure of it. But somehow they never quite added up to the right whole.

Frustrated, I smudged the latest attempt with my thumb, and left it that way, like her face was cast in shadow.

I sighed. I didn't feel much better, but at least I wasn't a shaky mess anymore. I threw my sketchbook back into my bag and dragged myself to my feet. I powered up the GPS app on my phone to check that Kelsey had made it home okay, determined to focus back on the task at hand.

When I saw her location, I groaned.

I wasn't sure if she'd ever made it back to her hostel, but she definitely wasn't there now.

5

DRESSED IN SWEATS and tennis shoes, I jogged the paths of the botanical gardens until I found her. Up on a hill overlooking the rest of the gardens, with purple flowers blooming on my left and the monastery spires rising up in the sky on my right, I almost missed her. She was sprawled out in the grass, facing the monastery. I ran past her, down the hill, and then stopped when I got near the bottom. I turned and walked back up, my hands on my head, pretending to cool down.

Kelsey was laid out on her side, and I might have thought she was sleeping if I didn't see her fingers picking at the grass. The rising sun glinted off the domes of the monastery, and when I reached the top of the hill, I walked another hundred feet or so past her before settling down on the trail. I leaned my back against a stone ledge just below the purple flowers, the blossoms nearly brushing the top of my head. I laid my elbows on my knees and sucked in a breath of crisp morning air.

Kelsey wore the same outfit as the night before. Her creamy lace skirt was short, showing off those familiar long legs. It was probably now covered in grass stains, but Kelsey didn't seem concerned. Probably the alcohol. She'd be pissed later. That peek of shoulder was catching the early morning sunlight, and I found myself dying to know what had happened between now and when I left her.

I grabbed my sketchbook again, and started with the monastery. With just a pencil, I had no way to capture the vivid colors, but I did my best to show the way the sunlight glinted off the gold spires and accents on the building. I worked on the sky and the flowers in the foreground before moving on to Kelsey.

At least this time, I didn't have to attempt to draw her face, only her silhouette. I couldn't have orchestrated a better pose for her if I'd tried. Lying on her side, she lined up with the horizon. Past the monastery, I could see the river, bridges, and the center of Kiev. It was almost as if those things bled out of the curves of her body.

I couldn't make up my mind who Kelsey Summers was. With how much she'd had to drink last night, I would have thought she'd be crashed out for half the day. But instead, we were here watching the sunrise.

As my pencil dipped to draw the curve of her waist, flaring out into her hips, I was reminded of an hourglass. Not just because of her perfect body. On its side, like Kelsey lay, an hourglass was stuck, moving neither forward nor backward, frozen in time. I'd been in that place before. Stagnant and lost, and I wouldn't have been surprised to learn Kelsey felt the same.

Maybe she'd found the magical balance that I'd never

been able to obtain. Maybe she could drink and party all night without getting sucked into the darkness that came with that lifestyle.

I wanted to believe that. But that could have been the addict in me, eager to insist that I could find that balance, too.

But I couldn't. And I didn't think Kelsey could either.

No one retreats to the bottle every single night unless they're running from something. And when you're running, you don't realize that to drown your troubles, you have to drown yourself, too.

AFTER KIEV CAME Bucharest, which passed in a blur of nightclubs.

She's stuck, I found myself thinking again as we repeated the same patterns.

More people spoke English, which made keeping up with Kelsey a little easier. But there were more pickpockets and con artists, which left me in a constant state of agitation, imagining all the ways Kelsey could get into trouble.

Tonight, at least, we ended up at a place with live music. That gave me something to focus on besides alcohol. Granted the music wasn't in English, but the beat was good. The guy on drums definitely had skill.

I turned my back on Kelsey, who was getting cozy in a corner booth with some guy she'd met at the hostel.

I rolled my eyes and settled in for a long night. Since arriving in Bucharest, we'd seen very little of the city. I'd bought another guidebook, hoping Kelsey might do some real traveling this time around. So far, though, I'd had nothing but a few glimpses of landmarks as I followed Kelsey around. Needless to say, it was beginning to get old.

"You understand this?"

A little brunette in an even littler black dress sidled up next to me.

"Not a word," I replied.

"Didn't think so."

I smiled. "What gave me away?"

"I might have seen you earlier. I think we're staying in the same hostel."

"Oh?"

Damn. I'd taken a chance and gotten a bed in the same hostel as Kelsey. The place was huge, and I figured I could stay under the radar. But if this girl recognized me, then I wasn't doing a very good job.

"Is that creepy?" she asked. I wasn't exactly qualified to talk about what was and wasn't creepy in that moment. "Sorry. It's just . . . my friends and I were looking for a place to sit. I thought maybe we could join you."

I looked back in the direction she had, toward the bar, and saw two other girls. That was certainly one way of occupying myself. It would keep me from contemplating the dangerous mystery that was Kelsey Summers. And the known danger of the bar.

"Sure. That'd be fine."

She waved at her friends, and then I was surrounded by

significantly more estrogen. She slid onto the seat closest to me, and I caught a whiff of sweet perfume.

"I'm Sarah. This is Johana and that's Christine."

Sarah reminded me a bit a doll—small, almost porcelain-like.

"I'm Hunt. It's nice to meet you all."

Sarah raised an eyebrow at my name, but didn't comment. I was used to that. And yeah, it would probably be less hassle to go by my first name, but Jackson felt like a different version of me, a version that I needed to maintain distance from if I were going to survive this job. Hunt was the version of me that had gotten his life together, and that's who I needed to be.

"Where are you from, Hunt?"

"Texas. Mostly. What about you?"

"New York."

"All of you?"

It was Johana who answered this time, the slight curl of an accent at the ends of her words. "Well, we all go to NYU. I'm originally from Paraguay."

The third girl, Christine, shrugged. "Kansas."

Sarah chimed in. "We're all studying abroad in the Netherlands. We're just visiting for the weekend. What about you? Studying abroad?"

I laughed and scratched the back of my neck. "No. I'm, uh, just traveling."

I'd never gone to college at all, let alone in another country, a fact that my father was quite fond of bringing up.

"That's cool," Sarah said. "So what have you done in Bucharest so far? Anything you recommend?"

I racked my brain for locations from the guidebook. "Uh, you know. The usual. A few museums, a church or two, Victory Avenue. There's the Dracula castle, too. But that's outside the city."

That wasn't too bad. Better than telling her what I was actually doing here in Bucharest. She directed her eyes toward the table, tapping glossy fingernails against the surface.

"And what are you doing tomorrow?"

I glanced back toward Kelsey's booth out of habit, only to find it empty.

I stood, pushing my chair back from the table. A quick scan of the area didn't give me any glimpse of Kelsey, and she was kind of hard to miss.

"Excuse me, I have to—"

I didn't bother finishing my sentence before I walked off in the direction of the bar. I circled it once, catching Sarah's eye by accident. I'm sure I looked psychotic, but there wasn't time to think about that. When I didn't see Kelsey after another lap, I pulled the phone out of my pocket.

She was on the move.

I shot one more glance at Sarah. The band was playing a softer tune behind her. She was pretty. I could have used a night to let go of all of this mess and just talk to someone normal. To *be* someone normal.

Tonight was apparently not that night. I waved in an apology, and then made for the exit.

I followed the GPS back to our hostel, glad that I wasn't having to chase her to another bar. If she was calling it an early night, fine by me. I'd been averaging about three hours of sleep a night between her partying and my nightmares. I could use the extra rest.

The hostel was split up dorm-style. I'd chosen one of the male-only rooms, which had about ten beds packed into too-close quarters. One guy was already out for the night, but the rest of the room was empty. I grabbed my shower stuff, eager to follow his lead.

I slipped on a pair of rubber flip-flops, and hoped that by retiring early, I'd get a decent amount of hot water. This hostel had several floors, with a shower on each. Kelsey was in a room on the first floor, and I was on the second, so I let my guard down.

Yet another mistake.

I hung my clothes on the hook outside the shower stall, then pulled the curtain closed. I turned on the faucet, cramming myself into the far corner of the stall to avoid the flash of cold water that came out first.

When it got to be lukewarm, I decided that was probably as best as I was going to get for the night. I stood beneath the spray, letting it dribble down over my face, and congratulated myself on making it through another day.

That's what I was back to. Counting the hours of sobriety just like I had those first few months. It helped me focus, but seemed to make time move slower. Three more days.

I'd built up the one-year mark in my head as if things

would magically get easier once I passed that point. I knew they wouldn't. But I let myself pretend for now.

Quickly, I finished washing up. Then I grabbed the towel I'd slung over the wall of the stall, pulled it tight around my hips before sliding open the curtain.

A soft, lilting laugh traveled down the hallway, announcing company. I picked up my things to exit at the same time that a girl stumbled through the door, laughing. She gripped the doorframe with one hand, but her upper body tipped toward the floor.

"Hey, easy there."

I reached out to steady her, and realized who she was before my hand even touched the familiar curve of her shoulder.

"I'm okay. I'm good." She was still laughing, but even holding on to the doorframe, she couldn't seem to stand up straight. She tossed her hair back, and I directed my gaze away, like that would keep her from seeing me. That's when I caught sight of the guy behind her, the same one she'd been hanging around with at the club.

"I've got her, mate."

Australian. He was a traveler, too.

He gripped her waist, and she fell back into his body, her eyes closed. God, how drunk was she? I was torn between being worried for her and relieved for me. I don't think she'd even noticed me, which meant she was unlikely to remember me in the morning.

But . . . I couldn't not say something.

"Are you sure?" I asked. "She's pretty wasted."

"Pretty and wasted. Can't beat that combo."

My stomach turned, and my fists clenched.

Kelsey wobbled past me, and I almost reached out and grabbed her. I almost told the douchebag to back the fuck off.

God, I wanted to.

She was drunk. Too drunk. But she was also holding on to the guy's neck and leaning her face against his chest like she wanted to be there. I didn't have any right to tell her what to do. She had to make her own fucked-up decisions, just like I had.

So I let him pull her into one of the shower stalls, her delirious giggle echoing out at me even once I could no longer see her. Squeezing my eyes shut, I dragged a hand across my face, suddenly battling the urge to punch something.

A piece of clothing, her dress most likely, was tossed over and out of the shower. The water turned on a few seconds later, and I heard her squeal rupture into peals of laughter.

I forced myself to leave then, my gait wooden and stiff. I didn't know what the right thing was to do in this situation. I shouldn't give a fuck. But I did.

My fascination with figuring her out had began to mesh with my attraction to her, and now I couldn't tell the difference between the two anymore.

I had to think this through. If I went back in there and interrupted, I was definitely outing myself. It was one thing not to pay attention to a random guy you walk past. If I tore open the shower curtain and beat the shit out the guy she was probably having sex with . . . I had a feeling she'd remember that, no matter how much she'd had to drink.

How would I follow her after that, when she could recognize me from even the slightest glance? And as far as I knew, she might be sober enough to know exactly what she was doing. She could tell me to fuck off, and then I would have burned myself for no reason whatsoever.

No, it was better if I minded my own business. And yet, when I lay down to sleep a few minutes later, I couldn't stop thinking about the possibilities. What if that guy had gotten her drunk on purpose? What if he hurt her? That would be my fault.

How would I explain that to her father? How could I live with myself knowing I could have stopped that? I rolled out of bed and stood to go find her, and got halfway across the room before I ground to a halt.

Goddamn it.

So she was wasted. She'd been wasted a lot on this trip so far. And she'd hooked up with random guys regardless of her sobriety level. I was overreacting. Clearly, she knew what she wanted out of this trip, and I just needed to let her do her thing.

I took a deep breath.

I needed to relax. Normally, I would have reached for my sketchbook, but the last four drawings I'd made had been Kelsey, and I had no doubt what number five would be, too, unless I wanted to draw the pimply guy snoring in the bunk next to me.

No, that wasn't going to do the trick this time.

I stripped off my shirt, and ignoring the fact that I'd just taken a shower, I got down on the floor and started doing push-ups.

There was a sharp twinge of pain in the shoulder that I'd separated in Afghanistan, but it eased into a dull, familiar ache after a few reps.

I needed to tire out my brain, and the fastest way to do that was to tire out my body. So I bent my arms, my breath huffing out across the dusty floor, and then pushed myself upward. I did it again and again. I reminded myself of all the people who'd tried to help me when I'd been off the rails. They'd only pissed me off and pushed me farther away.

I did push-ups until my arms ached, and then I switched to sit-ups.

By the time I crawled back into bed for the night, I wasn't thinking about Kelsey or alcohol or the past. I was only thinking about sleep.

6

THE NEXT EVENING I followed Kelsey to the train station. As we approached, I immediately raised my guard.

It was just after midnight. Gara de Nord loomed ahead of us, but as we got closer, I couldn't help but pick out the dilapidated buildings that dotted the street. I was used to seeing a lot of people out and about, considering Kelsey frequented late-night businesses, but these streets showed a different side of city life. A man lay curled up on his side next to a metal trash can. I saw Kelsey pause, and mentally urged her to keep going. He was likely harmless, but these streets were dotted with beggars, and I'd read enough of my guidebook to know they were likely to try and take advantage of Kelsey if she acknowledged them.

After a few seconds, she kept walking, her eyes fixed on the train station up ahead. A few people called out at her as she walked past, but she kept her eyes forward. I breathed a sigh of relief, glad at least that I didn't have to worry about her behaving recklessly when she was sober.

Inside the station, the atmosphere was much less tense.

It was still fairly busy, with a few shops and fast-food restaurants still open for business.

I took a risk standing behind her in line, but I needed to know where she was going, and this was my best shot. She had a Eurail pass, as did I, which covered travel to most places in Europe. But if she was at the ticket counter that meant wherever we were going wasn't covered.

I was fairly certain she wouldn't recognize me from the night before. I didn't think she'd ever really looked at me, but I kept my baseball cap pulled low over my eyes just in case. She stepped up to the ticket counter, her Eurail pass and passport in hand.

I tried to listen for a clue to where she was going, but the attendant's voice was muffled by the glass, and with her back to me, I couldn't understand what Kelsey was saying either. I fidgeted, tapping my passport against my palm, trying to decide the best way to handle this. I could always wait and see what platform she went to, and then come back and buy my ticket based on that. But I didn't know how early she had arrived and didn't want to risk missing the train. The attendant next to Kelsey finished with her customer and beckoned me forward.

I hesitated. Standing next to Kelsey was riskier than standing behind her. And what if she'd already said her destination and I couldn't figure it out?

The attendant called out to me.

Panicked, I turned to the person behind me and said, "Go ahead. I need to, uh . . ." I held up my phone as an explanation.

I don't think the person behind me spoke English, but when I gestured for him to pass me again, he did.

Kelsey handed over some cash to the attendant, and he handed her a ticket in exchange. After retrieving her change, she nodded and then walked away. Her attendant waved me forward, and I hesitated for just a moment, making sure Kelsey was out of hearing range.

"Same as my friend in front of me," I said.

"Excuse me?" the man asked, his accent thick.

"I'm with the girl you just helped."

"Ah," the man nodded. I just hoped he didn't look behind me to see that Kelsey was long gone because that would certainly make him suspicious. "As I told her, there are no more sleepers for this train, only regular seats."

"That's fine."

"I also can't get you beside her. The nearest seat is a few rows back."

"That's great," I said a little too quickly. I hadn't thought about what would have happened if he'd sat me right beside her. But for once, the universe seemed on my side.

"All the way to Belgrade, yes?"

I nodded. "Yes, that's right." Where was Belgrade again? Serbia?

Just for once, it would be great if Kelsey would choose a country that I knew at least a little bit about.

I handed over a credit card in exchange for the tickets.

It looked like we'd be changing trains twice, both times in Bulgaria before heading into Serbia.

At least tonight would be a change of routine from our regular nighttime adventures.

MY BREAK FROM the clubs, however, was short-lived. As a city, Belgrade wasn't the most visually attractive place we'd been to so far. Most of the buildings were boxy and gray. But as it turned out, Belgrade was like the Eastern European epicenter of clubbing or something. That's where the city really hit its stride.

Unfortunate for me.

The first night we hit a place near Kelsey's hostel (this time, I went back to my original method of staying nearby). It wasn't dissimilar from the places Kelsey had visited so far, but everything about the place was louder—the music, the neon, the outfits. It was like the dial had been turned up on everything.

Including the women. I had never seen so many beautiful women in my life. Most of them were almost as tall as me (especially considering that nearly all were wearing heels). They had long dark hair, tanned skin, and a penchant for revealing clothing. I wasn't sure if that was just because of the summer heat or the style. Either way, I wasn't complaining. And when Kelsey started dressing to match, she definitely got her fair share of attention.

Her pale head stood out in the sea of dark skin and hair, and I watched men's eyes follow her everywhere we went.

The men . . . well, they made it pretty easy for me to blend in. I'd say more than half of them had buzz cuts like mine. I fit in so easily that people were shocked when they realized I was American.

On our second day in Belgrade, I spent the afternoon hoping Kelsey would find something else to do that night.

I'd hit my one-year mark and adopted a Serbian dinar as a replacement for the chip I would have gotten if I were back home. If there was ever a night that I deserved to have free of temptation, this was it. I'd thought reaching this milestone would make things easier. I could only liken it to climbing a cliff just to stand at the top and discover another one stretching up in front of you.

Was this what every year would feel like? Was this what the rest of my life would feel like? One goddamn cliff after another?

I wanted to do absolutely nothing. I wanted to hide out in my hotel room, in the dark, and maybe break a few things. But when Kelsey stepped out of her hostel that night in a glittering black strapless dress, I knew I wasn't going to get my wish. I pulled on some leather shoes and a button-up shirt. That was about as dressed-up as I was willing to get at the moment.

We bypassed the clubs near the hostel and headed for the river. I stayed a few blocks back, far enough that, if Kelsey turned around and looked, she wouldn't be able to make out much except the fact that I was a man. I kept my hand on my phone in case she turned and I lost track of her (which I did, twice).

When I found her the second time, I very nearly blew my cover. I was about to round a corner when I heard her voice. I stopped short, then edged closer and peered around a building to see her pacing along the sidewalk, talking on the phone.

When she turned her back to me, I slipped out onto the sidewalk and stood next to a bus stop. I could see her when she faced my direction, but the stop hid me decently well.

She said, "Things are fantastic, Bliss. I can't even tell you how much fun I'm having."

Her voice was enthusiastic, but there was a longing on her face that bordered on sadness as she spoke.

"Belgrade," she said after a pause. "No, honey. It's in Serbia. I'll get to London, eventually. Why? Do you want me to bring home a British boyfriend like yours so we can have accent-filled double dates?"

She laughed at something the other person said, and then pressed a hand to her chest like she was feeling for her own heartbeat.

"I miss you, too."

For a moment, that natural light that seemed to accompany her everywhere dimmed. I thought that if I were to try to draw her now, I'd *finally* be able to capture her. It was the longing in her face. That's what I'd been missing.

"Oh, you know me. I like to be the life of the party. Speaking of which, I should get back to it. Sorry I woke you up. Yeah. Yeah, I'll call again soon." She nodded, her bottom lip tucked between her teeth. She choked on a laugh that sounded closer to a sob. "Yeah, all the juicy stories. I promise. Yeah, good luck with the move. Everything is going to be great. I know it."

She hung up, and stood staring at the phone for a few seconds. She looked as if all the energy had been siphoned out of her and she was running on empty.

She closed her eyes and tilted her head up toward the sky, letting her hand with the phone drop down to her side. She sucked in a few quick breaths like she was trying not to cry, and then abruptly dropped into a crouch.

In her short dress and heels, she looked as if she were trying to curl into a ball right there on the street. She rested her elbows on her knees and threaded her fingers through her hair, and I very nearly went to her.

I'd suspected something was wrong. Known it even. But could it be that simple? If she missed someone back home, why was she here? Why keep putting herself through all this?

I was dying to know.

Just when I was about to step out from the bus stop's shadow, she stood, that empty expression gone from her face. She took a deep breath, shook her head, and pasted on a smile as if stepping onto a stage.

Then she turned and began walking again. I did what I always did. I followed.

When she approached the river and began walking down a ramp toward a giant boat, I sped up my walk. I was halfway down the ramp when she met who I assumed were bouncers, based on their dress and size. She opened a little black bag for them to inspect, and I joined the line behind her. There were two people between us, and by the time I walked onto the barge to discover a massive floating club, I'd lost her in the crowd.

Out on the river, it seemed about ten degrees cooler, but I took one look at the thicket of bodies and knew that coolness wasn't going to last.

I donned a scowl, and began squeezing my way through the throngs of people. My little GPS app did jack shit in a place like this. It wasn't exactly conducive to helping me find Kelsey in a sea of outrageously tall Serbians.

If I could just catch a glimpse of her . . . She should be easy to spot, but there were too many people.

After an hour of squeezing through nonexistent gaps on the dance floor, I started to worry. That phone call had done something to her. Made her emotional. And if I knew anything, it was that partying and emotions could be a combustible pair.

I checked my phone again, and as best as I could tell, Kelsey was still on the barge.

There were bar tables set up around the perimeters with waiters, and it was tempting to park myself there and wait. I edged closer to one of them, but by the look of it, you had to order drinks to keep the table. I didn't trust myself to order a drink just for show.

But being on the perimeter, I caught a glimpse of one of the waitresses opening up a heavy velvet curtain to what I assumed was a VIP room. She pushed the curtain behind a hook to keep it open while she entered the room with a tray of drinks.

I caught my first glimpse of Kelsey.

She was dancing alone in front of a muscular guy with a permanent scowl. Her hands drifted through her hair, pulling it up and off her neck, and she carried on dancing as though she weren't the only person in the room doing so. She crooked a finger at the angry dude, and though he leaned forward on his knees to look at her, he didn't stand to dance.

Kelsey moved closer, walking two fingers across his wide shoulders to coax him into standing. He ran his hands up the back of her legs, gripping her thighs just below the short hem of her glittering dress.

I already hated him.

Eventually, Kelsey managed to charm him up from his seat, and she pulled him past the curtain toward the main dance floor.

She tugged on his hand, smiled, and then faced forward.

That was when her eyes locked on mine.

7

Shit.

Her head tilted to the side, and her eyes squinted. I froze. She recognized me. That's what that expression had to mean. Maybe she hadn't been as trashed that night in the hostel showers as I thought.

She released the VIP guy's hand and started down the small set of steps that led to the dance floor.

My heart didn't hammer. It beat in slow, heavy beats like a bass drum. It had the same kind of echo, too. I could have turned away. It wouldn't have been hard to melt into the sea of buzz cuts and slip off the boat. She'd be confused for a little while, but eventually she'd assume it was the alcohol or that she'd been imagining it.

That's what I should have done.

Instead, I kept my feet planted. I pulled my hands from my pockets, flicking my fingers with anticipation. I *wanted* her to see me. If she saw me, I could talk to her. I wasn't sure what I would say—what I could say that wouldn't give away who I was and how much I knew about her. But I could finally get some answers. And maybe help give her some comfort, too.

She walked toward me slowly, one heeled foot in front of the other.

When she was a few feet away, she smiled and my heart abandoned it's slow and steady beat.

This was stupid and crazy and ridiculous.

My body didn't seem to care about those things.

I sucked in a breath as she stepped up to me and held it in . . . as she slid past me and leaned up to place a kiss on the cheek of an impossibly tall guy with short dark hair.

"Здраво!" The word she said sounded like *zdrah-voh*, and based on his reaction, I'd say it was a greeting.

I was positive when he returned, "Hello again, Kelsey."

I stumbled back, trying to put a bit of distance between us, and tried to place the guy. I didn't recognize him from the club the night before, so that meant she'd met him when I wasn't around. Maybe at her hostel. Or earlier in the night when I'd lost her.

The two began talking, but I didn't hear them over my own berating thoughts about my supreme idiocy.

She laughed, and the guy from VIP grabbed her elbow, tugging her away from the taller guy. I watched her introduce them, calm and cool as though VIP guy wasn't squeezing her elbow so tightly that it looked painful.

The other guy stepped forward like he was going to do something, but she flashed him a look and then shook her head, laughing. She wrapped an arm around VIP, and it diffused some of his tension.

Now I really hated this guy.

She shot her friend an apologetic look, and then pulled VIP away onto the dance floor.

Before, in the VIP room, she'd danced alone, carefree and vibrant as she always seemed at night, but I could see the cracks in that facade now. She turned her back to him as she danced, and closed her eyes. Her full lips pulled down in a frown, and her jaw clenched like she was struggling to hold something in.

It took me a second to place the expression, but eventually I matched it with her face that first day in the gardens. When she'd said goodbye to the guy she'd been with in the woods, I'd been seated on the stairs watching. She'd passed me, heading off into the woods. But before she passed me on the stairs, I caught her expression as she climbed the stairs. She had a smooth, angular face, but somehow then it had looked almost caved in by exhaustion.

She looked the same now.

From song to song, even that expression disappeared until she was blank, like that first faceless sketch I'd made of her.

Eventually, she pulled away from the guy she was dancing with, only to have him pull her back in, his hands possessive claws at her waist.

She smiled, her blank face long gone. Gesturing off to the left, she peeled his arms from her waist. She held out one finger like she'd be right back, but there was an angry sag to his mouth. She reached up and kissed that gash of a mouth, and he let her go, watching as she wove across the floor to the hall where the bathrooms were located.

I didn't think as I moved toward him.

I just remembered his ugly frown, and the way he'd gripped her elbow.

Standing in front of him, he paid me no mind, still watching her disappear down the bathroom hallway.

"Go back to your room upstairs."

He turned toward me, and said, "What?"

"Leave her alone."

He scoffed and rolled his eyes. He turned and started off in the direction that Kelsey had gone.

"Hey, I'm serious." I grabbed his shoulder and spun him back around. "Leave her the fuck alone."

"She have a golden pussy or something? Is that why everyone wants her?"

"She doesn't have anything where you're concerned. You're going to be gone when she comes back."

"No, asshole. You will."

That was really all the provocation I needed. I'd been itching to break something since this morning, and this guy had irked me from the moment I saw him. Maybe I couldn't hold a real one-year chip in my hand to distract me, but his face against my knuckles should do the trick.

He shoved my hand off his elbow, and I let him. Only then I brought it back in a fist and rammed it as hard as I could across his jaw.

Pain burst across my knuckles, followed by a shot of adrenaline that burned up my veins and set a fire in my chest. He swung back at me, and I ducked, ramming my shoulder up into his midsection. He coughed out a breath, and stumbled backward, his sagging mouth now an ugly, gaping hole.

He spit, and then came raging back at me. His punch was slow, and I leaned back, letting it pass in front of my face. I threw a left cross, letting my hips and shoulder push through until impact.

He went down hard, carving out a hole on the dance floor as he sprawled out beneath the flashing neon lights.

It felt fantastic. Until I turned around to find the bouncer who had been stationed out front when I came on board.

I WAS NURSING a bruised jaw and a busted lip of my own, courtesy of the bouncer, when my own phone rang. I was hanging out just down the riverbank from the club, keeping an eye out for Kelsey, and I hit answer.

"Hello?" I closed my eyes against the sting of my split lip and heard Kelsey's father on the other end.

"Hunt?"

"Yes, sir."

"I didn't expect you to answer."

"Why not, sir?"

"It's four in the morning there, isn't it?"

So it was. He was becoming accustomed to Kelsey's altered schedule.

"I'm a light sleeper," I answered.

"Good. Where are you now?"

"Belgrade, sir."

"Where the hell is that?"

"Serbia, sir."

"Why in the world is she in Serbia? What do you even do in Serbia?"

I really didn't think he wanted to know. "Sightseeing. The usual."

"That stupid girl is going to wind up kidnapped or something, and I'm not paying the ransom just because she decided to go off gallivanting in Third World countries."

I winced. Serbia might have been a little rough around the edges, but it was far from Third World. I knew that from experience. And though I didn't think Mr. Summers was serious about not paying a ransom, it didn't make me any more inclined to spill Kelsey's secrets to the guy.

"She's not going to get kidnapped. Serbia is much safer now than it was a few decades ago. Belgrade especially is as safe as most other European capitals. And I'm watching out for her. She's fine."

"When's she coming home? That's what I want to know."

"I don't know, sir. I don't really get close enough to her to have a conversation."

Ignoring that moment tonight when I'd wanted to.

I added, "You could always call her. Let her know you're worried. Maybe she'll come home sooner or choose a more *familiar* destination."

She clearly missed home.

Mr. Summers only gave a low grunt in response.

"Just don't let her pull any stupid stunts."

"Stunts, sir?"

He sighed, exasperated. "She's dramatic, like her mother. She does something stupid, and then always finds someone else to take the blame. She'll come home pregnant or gay and it will be my fault."

"How would that be your fault, sir?"

"It wouldn't be. It would be yours."

Now *I* was holding back a sigh.

"Of course, sir."

"Good. Good night."

He didn't wait for my reply before he hung up, and maybe I was still looking for a fight, but I really didn't like him either.

I wanted to be relieved when Kelsey left the club a few minutes later without VIP guy, but that deflated look was back, and that didn't make me feel any better.

I followed her as she walked home alone, actively fighting the urge to jog up to her side and say hello.

There were a lot of things I didn't know about Kelsey Summers. But I did know that I was getting really tired of living on the sidelines.

8

KELSEY SPENT TWO more days in Belgrade, but I only saw her once. I'm not sure whether it was the phone call or the interaction with the VIP asshole, or something else, but she barely left her hostel.

At first, I thought maybe the GPS app was broken or that she'd left without her phone. I decided to head over and check just in case. Just as I was approaching the front desk to ask about her, she walked past in a pair of cotton shorts and a T-shirt.

If I hadn't spent so much time staring at her, I don't think I would have recognized her. Her hair was pulled up and wound into a knot on the top of her head. And she wasn't wearing any makeup. Her normally dramatic eyes were clean and bare. Her long eyelashes a dark blond.

She was still pretty, of course. But a different kind of beauty. It made me imagine lazy days in bed or movie nights on my couch. I thought of how it would feel to *be* with a girl like Kelsey, to have her comfortable enough with me that she didn't need the clothes and the makeup and the hair.

To have her be *mine*.

Somehow, I wanted this version of Kelsey even more, because she felt more real than every other version of her I'd seen so far.

I followed her to the grocery store. She didn't leave her hostel again until the day she checked out and headed for the train station once more.

In Budapest, it was like she hit the reset button. She was back to that vibrant character that drew everyone's gaze like a magnet. If possible, she seemed to have turned the volume up even further. Like each night had to outdo the one before it.

After a few days like that, though, I started to recognize patterns of her cycle. Just like before, she would get these quiet moments where she seemed to zone out and forget the part she was playing. Her face would go blank, even as her body kept dancing or partying or whatever.

And I could just tell; another crash was coming. I wondered how long it would take before she gave up trying to fool herself in the same way she fooled the rest of the world.

With another girl and three guys, they ventured into an area of Budapest away from the center of the city. The streetlights became fewer and farther in between, and there were empty storefronts and derelict buildings.

Kelsey didn't seem to notice. They'd already been drinking for a few hours.

But I was on high alert.

Since arriving in Budapest, Kelsey had been throwing

around money like it was nothing. Buying people drinks and dinner and whatever else it took so they'd treat her like the center of attention.

I was tired *for* her.

She just tried so damn hard, and I didn't understand why. She was gorgeous and vibrant, and she didn't need to do those things for people to want to be around her. She didn't need a lot of the things she surrounded herself with.

And throwing around money like that could have dangerous repercussions.

When the group led her into what looked like an abandoned building, my heartbeat thundered in my ears. I gave up stealth and sprinted after them, ignoring the careful distance I'd been trying to keep.

I threw myself through the front door and into a long, dark hallway. Music thumped, bleeding through the walls, and I sighed.

No danger. Just another party.

I followed the hallway until it opened out into some kind of secret bar, like the speakeasies that were popular during prohibition. You had to know where to look to find them.

The bar was a mix of mismatched furniture and odd décor. I imagined that they'd just picked up whatever other people threw out, and adorned the walls with the weirdest combinations that they could find.

It was definitely the most interesting bar we'd been in yet, and if this had been the first week of our trip, I might have entertained myself studying it all, but at this point, I could care less about seeing another bar.

All my attention was on Kelsey.

I didn't want her to crash. I thought back to that night in Belgrade, the way she'd just crumpled after that phone call. If that happened again . . . I would do something. I had to, right?

From my perch across the room, I watched her dancing with two of the guys she'd come with. When one of them went back to the bar, she wrapped her arms around the other guy's neck. When he leaned down to kiss her, I shifted uncomfortably.

Somewhere along the way, I'd given up trying to convince myself to treat this like a mission. It wasn't possible. She reminded me too much of myself before my fallout. And in letting go of that distinction, I had to embrace the one thing it had kept at bay.

Guilt.

Was protecting her a good enough excuse for prying into her life? For witnessing things that should have remained private?

I felt sick down to my bones, but I kept watching all the same, which is why I had a front-row seat for what should go down in the *Guinness World Records* book as the best way *not* to seduce a girl.

She tried to pull back from the kiss, and the guy sucked on her bottom lip like it was a lollypop. She made an expression of horror, and I couldn't help the laughter that ripped out of my mouth. She was always so calm and put-together and seductive, even when she was sad or drunk, but now her eyes bulged and her expression twisted in disgust.

It was fucking hilarious.

And when her eyes seemed to stick on me, while her bottom lip was stuck between his teeth, it was déjà vu. Like when I thought she'd seen me in Belgrade. I just assumed I was imagining it again. She finally managed to tug her lip free only for the guy to lick across her cheek. I held my abdomen, my muscles cramping from the first good laugh I'd had in ages. If every night were like this, I could handle her nightly bar crawls a lot easier.

Though those bar crawls would probably stop happening if every guy were like him. Her look of horror shifted from the guy in front of her to me, her eyes swooping down to scan me from head to toe.

Again, I told myself I was imagining it.

She made an excuse to get away, shouting "Toilet!" at the top of her lungs to be heard over the music. Almost as if it were choreographed, every head in the vicinity turned to look at her, but she turned to look at me. The laugh curled up and caught at the base of my throat.

I looked around, and with my back to the wall, there wasn't anyone else in the vicinity she could have been looking at.

I wasn't imagining anything.

She saw me. *Really* saw me.

She threw her hands up in the ultimate fuck-it-all gesture, and I found myself stepping forward as she exited the dance floor. I told myself it was because of the slight sway on her feet, that I was staying close because she was drunk.

The building was partially demolished in places, including the wall that had been knocked down between the bar area and the dance floor. In dangerously high heels, Kelsey tried to walk over the rubble that had been left behind. Her foot slid in her shoes, and her ankle turned sideways.

I thought she was going to do a face-plant directly on the rubble, so I rushed forward. At the last second, she balanced herself with a hand and then slumped into a sitting position.

I should have backed away.

But then she'd already seen me. And maybe this was my shot. To get some answers. To know her. To *help* her.

"What?" I asked, fully prepared to see her pouting up at me. "No more locals around to carry you?" Did that make me sound creepy, that I'd seen one of those Hungarian guys pick her up and carry her over the rubble earlier? Or did I just sound like an asshole?

Both. Probably both.

She looked up at me, and her eyes were dilated in the dim room, that ring of green barely perceptible even though I stood only a few feet away.

She straightened her shoulders and tipped up her chin. "I don't need anyone to carry me." Her hands roved over the rocks until she found purchase and started to push herself up. "I'm perfectly—whoa." She tilted sideways, her ankle rolling over again and she plopped down on her ass, harder this time. She held her hands up close to her face like she'd hurt them, and I had an indistinct urge, like a tugging at my middle, to *do* something.

Before she could really hurt herself, I stepped closer, finding a steady place to plant my boot. I hooked an arm underneath her knees, slipped the other around her back, and pulled her up into my arms. Her head lolled back, bumping against my bicep, and then I could feel her breath grazing my neck.

I clenched my jaw and focused on getting through the opening into the room with the bar. She gripped the back of my shirt near my shoulder blade, and the light touch coupled with the way she was staring at me, made a storm of curses rise in my mind.

You're one stupid man. Fucking stupid.

"You remind me of God," she said.

I laughed. Is that how she ended up with a different guy falling all over himself every night? Playing upon their God complexes?

"Well, that's a new one for me."

Unless you count—Jesus Christ, get a job. Jesus Christ, grow up. Jesus Christ, you're a disappointment. Those were familiar sentiments from my past.

She squinched up her eyes and shook her head in a way that made her look younger and made me want to laugh again.

"I meant . . ." Her frustration was almost endearing. "Let me down. I don't need anyone to carry me."

And we were back to abrasive. I wanted to tell her to shed the spoiled exterior because I *knew* there was something more underneath. But I couldn't say that. That was exactly what I *couldn't* say.

"I don't care what you think you need."

She rolled her eyes and then nuzzled her head into my shoulder. "Fine, carry me all night. Works for me."

God help me, but I was both annoyed and attracted to her. I always had been drawn to things that were bad for me, and she would definitely top that list.

Before I could do something stupid, like lean down and capture that stubborn pout with my lips, I dropped the arm that held up her knees and made her stand up on her own.

She gave me a small almost-scowl, but then shrugged in disinterest and began to flounce away.

"What? No thank-you?"

She stared at me over her shoulder and said seriously, "I'm not in the habit of thanking people who do things to me against my will. So, if you don't mind—"

She turned, ignoring me, and signaled for the bartender.

I hesitated. I could leave now and take my chances that she would only remember me in passing, not enough to severely hinder my job. She'd had enough to drink that that might be likely.

Or I could stay because . . . Well, I didn't have shit on the because side of things. My feet were already moving forward, and I'd already pulled out a stool to take a seat beside her. Because I *wanted* to.

"Give her a water, too," I said to the bartender.

She glared at me like I said, Give her the plague while you're at it.

I was a masochist. Really. That was the only explanation. You'd think voluntarily going to war would have taught me that; but no, staring into her eyes was when it became truly evident.

"You're awfully pushy, stranger."

She bit her lip, and her eyes wandered down the muscles of my arms, and I was glad I was sitting down because my body liked that entirely too much. I directed my eyes to the worn wood of the bar that looked like it had been repurposed and put together from scraps.

"You're awfully drunk, princess."

I needed to keep reminding myself of that.

She laughed. "Honey, I'm barely getting started. When I start talking about how I can't feel my cheeks and get a little touchy-feely, then you'll know I'm *awfully drunk*."

I'd seen her be touchy-feely, and then some. And the thought of being on the receiving end of that made the temperature seem to rise a few degrees.

The bartender returned with a shot of tequila, a slice of lemon laid across the top of the glass, and a cup of water.

Kelsey shot me a look of mock disdain and pushed the cup in my direction. I squeezed my hand around it as she took hold of her shot, offered me a sarcastic salute, and then tipped it back.

It was one thing to watch her drink every night from

afar; it was harder to be there right beside her. She'd thrown back the tequila without even a wince. In fact, I think she smiled as she bit into the slice of lemon. I stared at the empty shot glass she placed on the table, just the barest trace of tequila settling back down to the bottom.

To distract myself, I said, "If you're trying to drink away the memory of that kiss on the dance floor, I doubt it will work. That's the kind of kiss that sticks with you."

She made a face. The kind of face most people make after a shot of tequila. "You don't have to tell me that." She rubbed her knuckles across her cheek, no doubt remembering the path her *friend* had licked out on the dance floor.

I felt the need to laugh again, but stifled it. I didn't know what it was about this girl that was so funny to me. Maybe it was just that I saw a previous version of me in her, and I was finally starting to get enough distance from that version that I could see the absurdity in it all.

Kelsey's eyes locked on mine, and suddenly things seemed much less funny.

She said, "You know, you could always help me find another way to erase the memory of that bad kiss."

I closed my eyes with one thought. *Masochist.*

I slid off my stool and turned around, leaning against the bar. This way I could talk to her, but stare out at the dance floor.

I said, "I *could* do that . . ." But then I was certainly, completely fucked and wouldn't have a chance at following her without being recognized.

"But it's so much more fun to keep picturing the look on your face as it was happening."

She made an almost identical look of horror before settling into a pout, and this time I didn't manage to stifle my laugh before it escaped.

She leaned into me, her chin tipped up toward me. Her warm arm brushed mine, and I thought, who was I kidding? I was already fucked. I might as well pack my bags now.

She said, "I can think of a few things that would be *more* fun."

I looked over at her, even though I was supposed to be looking at the dance floor. I berated myself to look away even as my gaze trailed up her legs. It wasn't like I hadn't seen her before, in much less clothing even. But something about the fact that she was right in front of me, within touching distance, and that she *knew* I was looking made it even harder to look away.

When I got to her chest, a vision of that emerald green bra from the botanical gardens in Kiev popped into my head. I yanked my gaze away, my thoughts squealing like a train dangerously close to derailing.

A thought was forming in the back of my mind. An incredibly dangerous thought.

What if I didn't *have* to follow Kelsey?

What if I traveled *with* her?

I heard Kelsey huff beside me. "Well, this has been *interesting*. I better get back—"

No. She couldn't leave.

"To the dementor out on the dance floor? Really?" I might have protested a bit too quickly there, and she must have known it.

She took a few steps, her hips swinging and smiled. "You got a better offer?"

Did I?

One part of me screamed, "Hell, yes," while the other was busy urging me to pull away. I leaned toward her, but my fists stayed clenched on the bar top behind me, locking me in place.

Starting something with her would end badly no matter how I planned to proceed. I couldn't follow her anymore for fear of being recognized. And I couldn't travel with her because not a single guy she'd met so far had made it to day two with her.

So, no. I had nothing I could (or should) offer to her.

I slumped back against the bar, silent.

She followed my retreat, stepping up toward me and laying a hand on my chest. My muscles flexed involuntarily, and I had a very hard time remembering the argument I'd laid out only seconds ago in my head.

What if I *could* manage a second day with her? And a third? Maybe even more?

While I was struggling to maintain my control, she pulled the cup of water between us, wrapping her full lips around the straw. She took a long drink, and my blood migrated south.

I cleared my throat, not to say anything but because I needed something to *do* to keep from dragging her lips to mine.

She said, "Let me know if you change your mind."

I was changing my mind every 2.3 seconds.

And while I struggled with my thoughts, she sashayed back to the dance floor, back to the Hungarian guys I could have stolen her away from.

9

I WATCHED KELSEY dance with another local guy from the group she'd come with, and she was a force to be reckoned with. I didn't know how anybody said no to her. She closed her eyes as she danced, and she was magnetic as always—drawing more than just my stare.

I turned, tearing my eyes away, and realized where I'd been left. Alone. The bartender came up, mixing a drink, but looking at me in question.

I opened my mouth.

I thought about ordering a beer. Would a beer really be so harmless? As long as I stayed away from the strong stuff . . .

No.

Goddamn it. No.

I shook my head at the bartender. "I'm good. Thanks."

And then I shot out of there, needing to put as much distance as possible between me and the bar.

I chose a spot in the first room, where I entered the building. It was a little more low key, and I figured I could just station myself there for the rest of the night. I was close to the exit if I needed some air, but it was also a prime spot to wait for Kelsey.

With distance from the bar and from her, I was able to think a little bit more clearly. Though that didn't make what I should do any more evident.

I hadn't left myself with many choices.

I was still thinking about them when Kelsey came barreling by a few minutes later. Bracing a hand on the wall as she walked, she looked upset, so I followed. Ahead of me, she stumbled out onto the street, sucking in air like she'd just run a marathon. Then she doubled over and was sick on the street.

Fantastic.

That was one way to help me stay away from her.

Except . . . damn it.

I stepped up and pulled the hair back from her face. It was the least I could do. When she looked back at me, though, she gave me a look that said I was the last person she wanted to see.

"You okay?" I asked.

"I'm fine."

She pushed away from me, her hair slipping through my fingers as she tottered out into the street.

"Where are you going?"

She didn't look back at me as she answered, "Away. Just away."

She walked down the middle of the street, her hands out at her sides like she was prepared to catch herself if she fell. Follow at a distance? Or stick with her?

Like there was really a choice there.

"Hold on," I said, jogging to catch up.

As I overtook her, coming to a stop in front of her, she perched her hands on her hips. "Seriously?"

I pulled my lips into a thin line, understanding her incredulity. I couldn't believe I was doing this myself, but something about the image of her walking away from me had snapped something inside. I'd had enough of watching her from a distance.

"I'm not letting you walk around by yourself."

Never mind that I *couldn't*.

She crossed her arms over her chest, and her surprise melted into agitation.

"I told you, I'm *fine*."

I didn't believe her. Hadn't for a while now.

"Bad things happen every day to people who are fine."

And didn't I know it. You don't go into the military expecting to escape unscathed. Hell, a part of me had always thought I'd be one of the ones to never come home. The reality had been much worse.

"Listen, I get the whole protective thing," she said. "It's what guys like you do. And don't get me wrong, it's kinda hot." That should *not* have made my blood rush faster. "But I don't need a babysitter." I barely contained my laugh. "So put the knight-in-shining-armor fantasies on hold for the night."

I channeled my laugh into a roll of my eyes. I was no knight. And between the two of us, she was the one covered in armor.

"And I already told *you* that I don't care what you think you need."

I was paid to ignore that.

"So, *what*? You're going to follow me whether I want you to or not?"

I smirked, because the universe definitely had a sense of humor. It was a dark one, sending me of all people to look after a girl like her, but it was a sense of humor all the same.

"That's exactly what I'm going to do. Someone needs to get you home."

She scoffed and skirted around me. "I'm not going home yet. So run along and find yourself another damsel."

I took a frustrated breath and hid it behind a smile. She reminded me so much of myself, it was like looking in a mirror. A mirror I wanted to shatter. She walked away, and I called out after her. "You're a real piece of work."

I'd thought the same thing about myself on a daily basis once upon a time, until I'd had enough to drink to stop caring.

She spun around, walking backward, with a giant smile. She stretched out her arms displaying how much she didn't actually give a fuck and said, "You bet I am."

It would have made a great exit if she didn't stumble on her next step. I darted forward, but she caught herself on her own. Without sparing a look at me, she continued forward, walking a little faster.

Knowing it would drive her mad, I caught up and fell

into step next to her. She glared at me and tried to walk faster, but my legs were longer than hers. For a moment, I thought she might run just to leave me behind. Instead, she asked, "What's your name?"

Not what I expected.

"You waited long enough to ask that."

In fact, I was damned surprised I hadn't given myself away already and called her by name.

She shrugged. "Names aren't exactly the important bit in places like this." She waved a hand back in the direction of the bar we'd left. "And, honestly, I couldn't care less."

"So, then, why ask? If names aren't important and you don't care?"

"Well, first, we're no longer in said bar. And second, you're following me, and I'm asking questions to fill the silence, because otherwise things will get awkward. And talking keeps me from thinking about how you're probably a serial killer, hence the whole following thing."

Well, at least she wasn't completely oblivious to her safety. Though, if I did mean to harm her, asking my name wasn't going to stop me.

"From a knight in shining armor to a serial killer."

She bounced one shoulder in a shrug. "The nice-guy bit could be an act. And you definitely look like you could be dangerous."

I was. And not just because of my training. Kelsey might be wild, but the old me still could have put her to shame. And if I fell off the wagon, I could easily drag her down that road with me.

"Are you always this honest?" I asked.

"Not even close. It's the alcohol talking. Totally powers down my filter."

Good to know.

"I'll tell you my name if you'll tell me something about yourself."

I had only facts on a paper and observations that I tried incredibly hard to keep from morphing into the worst assumptions.

"Like what?"

"It doesn't matter. Something else honest."

She paused for a few moments, her steps faltering. She veered sideways, her shoulder brushing my arm. I held out a hand ready to catch her if she fell, but didn't touch her yet.

"Honestly? . . . I'm tired."

I laughed. I asked for honesty, and I guess I got it.

"That's because it's almost dawn."

"Not that kind of tired."

"What kind of tired, then?"

"The bone-deep kind. The kind of tired that sleep doesn't fix. Just tired of . . . being."

For a few moments, I was shocked into silence. I'd known there was something more going on in her head. I'd wanted to crack open her facade and find the truth beneath it. But I didn't feel any better having my suspicions confirmed. In fact, I felt infinitely worse, sickened by the worn look on her face and frustrated by my inability to fix it.

"You don't show it." Not to most people anyway, but I was the one person who saw when no one else was looking.

"I don't show much of anything."

Damn. For all my desire to unravel her secrets and excavate her issues, I wasn't sure that I wanted to know now. I already felt too much for someone who was supposed to be my unbiased mission, and knowing what hurt her would only dig me deeper.

"I bet that gets tiring, too."

She sucked in a breath and raised her chin like she was going to nod, but then she stumbled, one of her heels sticking between the cobblestones. I caught her up to my side, squeezing her a little closer than was probably necessary.

How drunk was she now? She had to be sobering up.

"How are your cheeks?"

She blinked a few times, and the fist at my shoulder uncurled, fingertips pressing into my muscle.

"Can you feel them?" I added.

When she still didn't react, my traitorous hand drifted up, and I brushed my fingers across her cheek.

"They, um, just feel a bit heavy is all."

I stared into her eyes, wondering if I might find some of those secrets I craved and dreaded, there in her gaze. As it turned out, it didn't matter whether she was dancing or smiling or frowning, she was still magnetic.

And I didn't want to resist it anymore. But I had to.

I made sure she was steady on her feet and then let go.

"Your turn," she said.

"My cheeks feel fine."

She shook her head, smiling. "I meant your name."

I kept walking, determined to just get her home.

"Most people call me Hunt."

Everyone called me Hunt except my family. I don't know why I hadn't just told her Hunt straight out. Maybe I wanted her to know some of my secrets, too.

"Should I call you that? Am I most people?"

I fisted my hands in my pockets and picked up my pace. "Honestly, I have no idea what you are."

And it was driving me *crazy*.

We didn't talk much after that. She turned at random, and so did I, trying to subtly steer us in the direction of her hostel in the central part of Budapest.

Around sunrise, we hit the Danube, which meant we were close.

I didn't realize she had stopped until I'd already passed her. I stopped and looked back at her. She was holding her breath, gazing at the sunrise with renewed energy.

She pointed south. "There's a club a little ways that way that's open until six."

She needed to rest. And so did I. And I was scared of what I might let myself do if I went to a club with her. "I think you've partied enough tonight."

God, I sounded like such a buzzkill. But it was true. If she hadn't managed to chase away her demons for the night, more alcohol and dancing wouldn't help. She just needed to sleep it off.

She didn't answer me. Instead, she stepped out into the

street and crossed toward the river. She hadn't even bothered to walk at a crosswalk. I glanced around, checking for cars. There was one coming, though still far away.

"Where are you going?"

She turned, walking backward again in the same way she did when she'd nearly fallen earlier. "Absolutely no idea."

I heard the thrum of an engine, and knew that car was getting closer, moving fast.

I ran for Kelsey, who was now just standing in the street. I dragged her up onto the sidewalk, my heart beating a little faster.

"Are you crazy? Don't walk across a fucking road without looking where you're going!"

She jerked away from me. "*Relax.* I'm fine. There's no one out this time of morning anyway."

The car stole past, a sleek black sports car. Two-seater by the look of it. I tried not to look smug.

Kelsey's lips puckered. "You don't have to say it." She started jogging toward the river. "I'm a piece of work. Got it. But you know what?" she shouted louder. "I'm *so* good at it."

I followed close behind. When she started slipping off her heels, I wasn't sure whether her feet were hurting or if she was planning to dive into the Danube. She lifted her arms into the air and screamed into the early morning air. A nearby group of birds took off into the sky, and she sucked in a lungful of air.

I watched her, fascinated. She was trying to get out

from under the darkness, that much was clear. She stands out in a crowd but, I wondered, how much more radiant she could be if she managed to get free from her demons.

"You're ridiculous," I said.

"Correction: I'm *fun.*"

She took off running, and I dragged my ass after her, a smile creeping onto my face. I was imagining what it would feel like to catch her, winding my arms around her waist and pulling her back against me, when she abruptly slowed to a stop.

I came up behind her, and one look told me where we were. I still bought guidebooks in every country, though I'd yet to have much use for them. I knew from my current book that this was the *Shoes on the Danube Promenade.*

"It's a Holocaust memorial," I told her. During World War II, a group of Jews, including some from the resistance, had been lined up by the river by a militia and ordered to take off their shoes. Then they'd been shot into the river. In memory of them, there are dozens of iron-cast shoes mounted by the water on the promenade.

She sucked in a breath, and that light she'd been trying to reclaim, that girl that had screamed at the top of her lungs just for fun, faded away.

Tragedy does that.

War does that.

I'd gone into it fully prepared to give up my life in the process. But war never gives you what you're prepared for. It takes pleasure in being unpredictable. No one ever expects to be a sole survivor. When things go wrong, you always expect that you'll go with the rest. Better to be gone in an instant in one well-timed blast than to fade away slowly.

I knew—logically, I knew—that those iron shoes were old-fashioned styles that were over half a century old. But when I looked, they all seemed to morph into the familiar marine-issue boots of the unit, the family I'd lost.

War changes. It's fought with different weapons, in different places, by different people.

But it never gets any less ugly.

10

WHEN I PULLED my gaze away from those imagined boots, Kelsey's eyes were wide and glassy. She had that empty look again.

"Are you okay?"

She turned away from me, clearing her throat, and I wanted to pull her into a hug. I didn't. But I wanted to.

"Yeah, I'm fine," she said. A sentence I was getting used to hearing. "Just yawned. Maybe I'm a little tired after all."

Trying to make her more comfortable, I teased, "You mean I finally get to walk you home?"

She turned around, smiling and composed, but I could still see the heavy sag in her shoulders.

"Come on, then, Prince Charming. Let's see what this chivalry stuff is all about. I hear good things."

That might have been the moment when I stopped blaming her for dragging me to bar after bar in city after city. Not that it hadn't all been miserable as hell. But there was one difference between Kelsey and the way I'd been a few years back.

She *tried*. She tried so incredibly hard, which is more than I ever did.

So I smiled, and turned to walk her home.

"I haven't been called chivalrous in a *long* time," I said.

This time she looked before she crossed the road.

"Fine by me. Chivalry sounded pretty boring anyway."

I laughed because she was funny. Despite it all.

She met my eyes. "Tell me something. If you're not walking me home because it's the gentlemanly thing to do, why *are* you here?"

"Back on the serial-killer bent, are we?"

It was easier to joke than acknowledge why I was really there.

"Nah, you're not a serial killer. Too soft for that."

"Soft?"

She threw me a smile before turning onto the street with her hostel.

"Hold on, now. Did you just call me *soft*?"

I turned her around by her shoulder. Maybe I pulled too hard or maybe she wasn't quite sobered up yet because she planted a hand against my stomach to keep from falling into me.

I stiffened.

"Well, I wouldn't call *this* part of you soft."

She looked up at me through her lashes, her voice smooth, and want for her punched me in the gut, right where I could feel the heat of her hand bleeding through my shirt. She leaned into me, and the adrenaline pouring through me made everything except the beat of my heart go silent.

"Kelsey," I said. I was already too sucked in to push her away, but I tried to warn her off anyway.

She tilted her head to the side and said, "How did you know my name?"

Shit. Fuck. Shitty fucking shittery.

"That girl said it. The one you came to the bar with."

That answer wasn't any better. Now she'd know I was watching her long before I talked to her.

She reached up to my shoulder and smiled. She didn't look suspicious.

"Well, then, you know my name, and I know yours. How *else* could we get to know each other?"

Her hand slid up my abdomen to my chest, and I tensed, barely holding on to my control. I swayed toward her, touching her lightly just above where her waist was smallest. I wanted to touch her everywhere.

She gripped the back of my neck, bending my head down, and I flexed my hands, trying to stop myself from throwing her over my shoulder and taking her back to my hotel room.

She stood on her tiptoes, and her lips brushed my chin. It was a testament to how much I wanted her that I was a few seconds away from kissing her even though I'd watched her be sick on the street maybe an hour or two earlier.

Her shirt was bunched up in my flexed fists and the side of my hand grazed bare skin. I nearly lost it. I cast my gaze up to the sky and growled, *"Goddamn it."*

She wrapped her arms around my shoulder, and then reached a hand up to tip my head down toward hers. I let her, even though I was shouting inside to walk away. I was thinking with my dick instead of my head, and I needed to get that under control. I might not have known the real Kelsey, not really, but I knew her well enough to know that if we slept together tonight, she'd be done with me.

Then I'd lose this job and have to go crawling home back to Houston. Then *I'd* be the one on a downward spiral.

And what would happen to her if I were gone? Would her father send someone else in my place?

For some reason, the thought of someone else watching her and seeing her the way I'd seen her made me irrationally angry. If I was right about the cycle she was on, she needed someone to look out for more than just her safety, and I didn't trust anyone else to do that.

And if I was honest, I didn't want to leave. Not just because I didn't want to go home, but because I didn't want to leave her.

It was the fascination, I told myself. I didn't want to go until I knew her story, until I understood.

It was a good thing I was better at lying to her than I was at lying to myself.

Determined, I pushed her away.

Almost immediately, I wanted to pull her back.

Instead, I stepped away. "You should go. Get some sleep."

She was breathing heavy, and it drew my eyes to her chest, and *fuck*.

"What?" she asked.

"You've had a long night." That I would *not* make any longer.

She crossed her arms over her chest, and I knew that armor was coming back up. "That sounds an awful lot like chivalry to me. *Boring* chivalry."

I took another step back because she was still too close for comfort, and my control was a thin, thin line.

"This is you, right?" I asked, pointing to the hostel at her back, even though I knew it was.

"Uh, yeah, it is, but—"

"Good. Then I'll leave you alone."

I walked backward, my steps stiff. "Good night, Kelsey. Or Good morning."

Then I rounded the corner. I walked just far enough that she wouldn't be able to see me anymore, and then I sagged against the building.

Around the corner, I heard her say, "What the fuck?"

What the fuck, indeed.

I TOOK A long ice-cold shower that night back in my room, mindful that I had crossed enough lines for the evening to not repeat my shower fantasies of her. Then I crashed, glad for the oblivion.

I woke sometime later, the sun bright outside my window and my phone ringing. Bleary-eyed, I answered, "Hello."

"Mr. Hunt. I see Kelsey is still spending a small fortune."

I sat up in bed, suddenly alert.

"Uh . . . yes, sir." How else was I supposed to answer that?

"Well, get me up to speed."

I swallowed. "Not that much to tell, sir. We're in Budapest, Hungary. She's safe."

"Yes, but what's she *doing*? Where is all that money going?"

I hesitated. "Uh, lots of things."

"Spit it out, Hunt."

"Dinners," I answered. "She meets people, and they go out to dinner. Touristy stuff. Museums. Plays. Lots of souvenirs."

"Really?" He didn't sound like he believed me.

"Clothes, too." I added for good measure. "Expensive ones."

"Of course." *That* he believed me about. "Right, well, I have a meeting. You'll let me know if anything changes."

It wasn't a question.

"Yes, sir."

I hung up and immediately powered up my Kelsey app. I cursed when I saw she was already out and about for the day.

Did that girl *never* sleep?

After a quick shower, I grabbed my bag and set off in search of her. I expected to find her carbo-loading to fight a hangover (or maybe that's just what I would have been doing).

Instead, she was having another one of her quiet moments. Large coffee in hand, she was seated on a park bench in a busy neighborhood square. She wore a light sundress, and her hair was as styled and perfect as ever.

She didn't look tired, not in the slightest.

I parked myself under the shade of a tree off to her left, far enough away that the busy sidewalks should hide me.

She sipped her caffeine in quiet contemplation, studying a fountain in the middle of the square. I didn't remember it from the guidebook, but told myself I would look it up later. For now, I pulled out my sketchbook.

On the walk over, I'd started thinking about all the drawings I'd done during our trip so far. A few were from landmarks I'd seen in passing, but most were of Kelsey. I still hadn't been able to get her face just right, so I'd stuck to sketching her in profile when I could.

Most of my drawings I did after the fact, when I couldn't sleep or while sitting around in a bar. I wasn't about to pass up the chance to draw her in real time. Maybe that combined with getting to meet her last night would finally help me get the face right.

I zoned out, sketching first the fountain and then Kelsey.

I'd never been trained in art. I mean, I'd taken a class or two in high school, but I hadn't exactly paid attention. I'd been preoccupied with other things then and drawing still lifes of fruit hadn't been all that appealing.

I was observant, though, and I taught myself. I'd had a lot of time for trial and error, too. I'd seen plenty of action in Afghanistan, but there'd also been a lot of sitting around waiting, doing nothing.

When I got to Kelsey's face, I contemplated everything I knew about her: that familiar empty sadness that shone through on occasion, her admission from last night that she was tired, "bone-deep" as she'd put it. When I drew her with that in mind, overlaid with a smile, the drawing came to life.

She was frailer in the drawing than she appeared at first glance, but it worked. Her hair and dress blew in the wind, and she clutched that cup of coffee like a lifeline.

I was probably reading too much into this, projecting my memories of myself onto her, but Kelsey was more than just tired. She was sad. And I was desperate to know why.

When I looked back at her to put some finishing touches on her dress, she was gone. My eyes darted around and found her closer to the fountain, amidst a group of pre-teen boys.

A bigger boy was holding a book over the water, taunting a younger kid, and I watched Kelsey play him. She pretended to need directions, and then when she had the opportunity, she took the book.

She gave it to a scrawny boy in the group who looked at her like she was descended from heaven. She kissed his cheek, and the kid's face split open in a smile. Whatever she'd done, she'd just made that kid's world.

I was a little jealous.

And my *fascination* with her was raging like a wildfire.

Her good deed done, she headed for the crosswalk at the corner of the street. I went to the opposite corner and crossed to the other side of the street, thinking I might have better luck following her undetected from there.

I couldn't help but notice that her shoulders were a

little straighter and the smile on her face didn't disappear once she'd left that boy behind. I found myself smiling in response.

I was right about her being even more brilliant when the darkness wasn't hanging over her. It was like the sun had appeared from behind the clouds, and I couldn't have looked away if I tried.

11

MAYBE MY MIND had always been made up, but when I followed Kelsey to some kind of rave at one of Budapest's famed thermal baths the following night, I knew I wouldn't be able to stay away from her.

She wore this intricate black swimsuit that wrapped around her body, accentuating the slim circle of her waist before it tied onto her bikini bottoms at the hip.

She was stunning.

There was a lot to look at. Plenty of beautiful, barely covered women. Roman-style columns. Colored lights. Live music. Sideshow acts like fire breathers and a trapeze artist.

Still, I only watched her.

She was there with some girl she'd met in the hostel. They'd gone out to a bar crawl together the night before, and I kept my distance. Kelsey had seemed reserved. When she went home alone, an ugly knot of tension in my chest had unwound. And if her going home alone made me relieved, the thought of her with someone else burned my blood.

So when I saw her talking to a guy in the thermal baths, I didn't hesitate. I started making my way toward her. Her hand was on his shoulder, and even that drove me crazy.

She saw me, and then practically fell all over herself to put her back to me in the hopes that I wouldn't see her.

She wasn't going to get away from me that easily.

The girl from the hostel pulled her aside and then stared openly at me.

Did that mean she knew who I was? Did Kelsey say something about me?

The closer I got, the faster my blood pumped. Maybe it was her or maybe it was my secret, but the adrenaline rush was the most powerful one I'd had since I'd been discharged.

When I stood behind Kelsey, her friend was practically gleaming with excitement. I leaned down to her ear. A wisp of her hair tickled at my neck, and I said, "Nice to see you again, Kelsey."

She turned around, and I relished seeing her off-balance. More than that, though, her closeness was electrifying.

"How are your cheeks this evening?"

She cleared her throat. "Uh . . . good."

She just stared at me, like she couldn't quite believe I was there. I held back a smile. Reaching an arm out to introduce myself to her friend, I made sure to lean in close to Kelsey. Our skin brushed, and she sucked in a breath.

Chuckling, I shook her friend's hand.

"Hello, I'm Hunt. It's nice to meet you."

"I'm Jenny. Likewise. " She was pretty. She had a similar build to Kelsey's, but with dark hair and eyes. She could have passed for a local.

"Is that short for Hunter?" Kelsey asked.

I let go of Jenny's hand and looked down at Kelsey. I still wasn't quite used to having those brilliant green eyes directed at me. "It's not."

She watched my lips long after they stopped moving, and I nearly forgot all about why I wasn't supposed to kiss her. She made me forget a lot of things.

"So your parents just named you Hunt?"

"Not exactly."

"God . . . Vague much?"

She was frustrated. Good. That meant I wasn't alone.

"There you go calling me God again."

She shot me an exasperated look, and who knew that would turn me on?

Then her guy-of-the night moved right next to her, and that cooled my reaction. What if she was more interested in him? Not that she *needed* to be interested in me when I'd promised myself I wasn't going to act on it.

If this was going to work, we needed to be friends. Maybe she would travel with a friend. I only had the rest of our stay in Budapest, though, to convince her, because I couldn't *accidentally* run into her in whatever city she visited next, not without arousing her suspicion.

I glanced at the guy at her elbow and then the rest of the group she was with. "I didn't realize you were here with others."

Lie.

"You scared of a little competition?"

I laughed in lieu of an answer and was glad when she didn't even glance at the guy trying unsuccessfully to get her attention.

"What about your other friends?" I asked. "The ones from the other night?"

She shrugged. "We weren't really friends. But this is Jenny." She pulled the other girl closer. Was that nervousness that I detected? That was new.

"Yes. We met. A few seconds ago."

She blanched, and I enjoyed it entirely too much.

"Right. We're staying in the same hostel."

She jumped slightly, and I realized that the guy had touched her back. It was irrational and inappropriate, but I wanted to break his arms and use them as chopsticks. "Because we're *sisters*. And it makes sense for *sisters* to stay in the same place."

I raised an eyebrow. Sisters? Kelsey didn't need to try that hard to get a guy's interest. Hell, she'd had my interest when I didn't even really *like* her.

Jenny clapped her hands together. "Oookay, I believe it's time for drinks. I *know* I could use one . . . Kelsey?"

Kelsey looked at Jenny like she was the Second Coming. But then she looked at me, and she hesitated.

What did that mean?

Was it so obvious that I didn't drink?

She let out a slow breath.

"One drink," she told Jenny.

She moved closer toward me, and I knew by the look on the dude's face the second she passed out of his reach. Barely an inch separated her bare skin from mine, and I was buzzing with it.

"Come with me?" she asked.

There was a roar in my ears that shifted and settled in my chest. Despite my friendship plan, I liked it very much when she looked at me like that, her bottom lip caught between her teeth.

"I would have thought you had enough to drink the other night."

She frowned, and there I was, being an asshole again. I kept forgetting that she wasn't as familiar with me as I was with her.

"It's just one drink. My first of the night. Come have a little fun."

I hesitated. It had been so much harder to be close to her and alcohol at the same time. Like the temptation was magnified. If I kissed her, I could taste both of the things I'd forbidden myself to have.

She said, "Or I can just catch up with you later."

She leaned away, and I got over my hesitation pretty quickly. Temptation, be damned. I gripped her waist and pulled her back to me.

"Okay, let's go."

I stifled my thoughts of concern and told myself that I could handle it.

Her. The alcohol. All of it.

"Your new friend seems a little reluctant to leave you."

She looked ahead of us to where the other guy had now joined the group around her friend Jenny.

"He'll get over it. We literally met like two minutes ago."

"I know. I saw you when you came in."

Her head snapped toward me, and her expression was worth admitting that I'd been watching her.

"I really enjoyed that little spin move you did while you were trying to hide."

"I wasn't *hiding*. I just . . ."

She floundered, trying to come up with something, and it was so damn adorable.

"Okay." She rolled her eyes. "So I *was* hiding. It's not every day I make a fool of myself. I wasn't exactly excited about rehashing that."

"It wasn't that bad."

I didn't know why it was so much fun to rile her up. Call it payback for her unknowingly torturing me for weeks. Or maybe it was the fire in her eyes.

"What are you doing here?" she asked.

I raised my eyebrows in response.

"It's a room full of women in bikinis. What do you think I'm doing here?"

Her lips twisted into something resembling a pout.

"I meant what are you doing *here*? With me."

We reached the stairs leading out of the pool. She stepped up and out of the water, and seeing her slick skin, her suit clinging tight to her curves, was nearly the death of me. I was turned on, and there was no way she didn't know it.

Her nipples showed through the fabric of her swimsuit, and I wasn't sure whether that was from the cooler air or from me, but I knew which one I wanted it to be.

My throat was scratchy with desire as I asked, "What was the question?"

"I asked what you were doing here with me."

I sensed her nervousness again, and it went straight to my head.

"Oh, you mean you asked a stupid question?"

She frowned. "You still haven't answered it."

"Yes, well." I reached out one finger, trailing through the drops of water collecting along her collarbone. "You make it hard to think straight."

Her eyes lit up, and she pulled me after her. "Come on, soldier. You can finish staring at me at the bar. I promise I'm not going to disappear."

I took a deep breath and forced myself to look away from the curve of her ass.

"Stupid. So incredibly stupid," I mumbled to myself.

She led me to one of three bars that had been set up inside the domed thermal-bath building. The rest of her group had gone ahead of us and had already claimed a section of barstools. I gladly took a seat on one as soon as we were close enough.

Kelsey leaned over the bar, and I was exceptionally glad that I was sitting down.

"Gin bitter lemon," she told the bartender. Then she looked back at me. "What do you want?"

"Nothing. I'm good."

I took a deep breath. I had to stay good.

She rolled her eyes and said, "Make that two gin bitter lemons."

I swallowed. This was a bad idea. I should get up and leave now, make some excuse. But that swimsuit . . . Heaven help me, but I am a weak man.

I dipped two fingers under the strap at her hips and pulled her back toward me. She fit perfectly between my knees. Resting her elbows on my thighs, she leaned back into my chest, and I barely resisted planting my lips on her neck.

I could flirt with her without taking it too far. I wasn't in high school anymore. I had some control.

Needing to ease some tension, I said, "Whatever happens tonight—"

"Yes?"

"Don't throw up in the pool."

She pulled away from me, half scowling, half smiling. And even though my body ached at the loss of contact, I knew it was for the best.

I laughed, trying not to betray the tension that was plaguing me.

"Just for that, *funny guy* . . . you're buying."

When the drinks came, I did as ordered and rose to pay. She stole my stool while I did, and when the bartender handed over the drinks, it all felt too familiar.

I handed her a glass, and then began the worst battle with temptation so far. It was there in my hand, only inches away from my lips. And it would be so simple to let it happen. The memory of it was still trapped in my muscles, and I could feel them straining to lift the glass to my lips.

"So, Hunt. Where are you from?"

Distraction. Yes. Perfect.

"Where am I *not* from would be the easier question."

"Military brat?"

I wished. Dad just went where the money was.

Trying to keep things light, I said, "Are you calling me a brat?"

She crossed her legs, and my eyes followed.

"If I were going to call you names, *brat* would not be my first choice."

My fingers brushed her ankle. I told myself it was okay because it was distracting me from the drink in my hand. The lesser of two evils.

I said, "What would you call me, then?"

"Well, I've already called you soft." I tried not to groan at the memory of that night. If I'd thought leaving then was hard, tonight was going to be brutal. "But I'm not above admitting when I'm wrong."

My fingers drifted from her ankle up the back of her calf. She pointed her toe, and her leg bumped up against my hip.

"What brings you to Budapest?" I asked.

Her foot hooked around the back of my leg, her toes tickling the skin behind my knee. She smiled, all too aware of what she was doing to me.

"Nothing in particular. It just seemed like an *interesting* place." She used that foot to pull me forward, and I didn't resist. "What about you?"

I kept my touch light, even though I wanted to grip her legs and pull them open for me to slide between. "Following a whim," I answered.

Her tongue darted across her bottom lip, and I was a goner.

She said, "Do you ever get any less cryptic?"

"I thought women liked a mystery."

Her eyes were hooded, and I couldn't even bring myself to feel guilty about any of this.

"Women *love* a mystery. But only if we think we can figure it out. Are you going to let me figure you out, Hunt?"

She couldn't. Not ever.

I gripped the edge of her stool and leaned down to her ear. Her skin smelled salty and sweet. "That's a two-way street, princess."

And God did I want to figure her out, even though I couldn't return the favor. Not just her personality or her past. Every part of her. I wanted to know her like the back of my hand.

I was two seconds away from beginning that process, my eyes trained on her collarbone, the first place I wanted to taste. Then Jenny popped up right next to us.

"We're going back in the bath, you two coming?"

I pulled away. Damn it, I had to keep pulling away. That was too close. I took advantage of Jenny's distraction to place my drink on the bar, out of range.

Kelsey held up a glass that was still almost full and said, "We're still working on these. You guys go. Have fun."

After Jenny left, Kelsey took a sip of her drink, fixing her eyes on me.

It didn't take Kelsey long to notice the absence of my glass. "You've not touched your drink. I know it looks a little girlie, but I swear you'll like it."

I sat on the stool next to hers. "I'm okay. Really."

"Oh, come on." She jumped off her stool, and leaned her flat stomach against my bare knee. "Try mine."

I didn't know where to look. Her face, that glass—neither was safe.

"I'm fine."

"You're so serious. Loosen up a little. Have some fun."

She took another drink, and her tongue trailed her bottom lip again. The ache rose up in my chest—for her, for all of it. "Just try it. For me?"

She slid between my knees, and I settled my hands on her waist. To push her away. To pull her close. I didn't know.

I stared at her lips, imagining the sweetness of her mouth paired with the strong edge of alcohol.

I could stay in control for her.

One drink wouldn't kill me. And knowing I needed to watch out for her would help me keep it in check.

One drink.

One sip.

Just once.

I said, "If you'll answer a question for me."

She tilted her head to the side, and I reached out to trail a thumb along the slant of her neck.

"Deal." She smiled.

She took one more drink, and then slid the glass into my hand.

It seemed tiny. It was maybe half full. Nothing that would do me any harm. I looked back at her smile. Quickly, I pulled the glass up and took a short sip before holding it out to her. She gave me a look. I could have brushed it off. But really, the drink hadn't been that strong. Like lemonade, but a bit more sour.

I brought the glass up and took a longer drink this time. When I gave it back, there was nothing but ice left.

She smiled, her lips close to mine.

"My turn," I said. "The other night . . . what did you mean when you said you were tired of being?"

She froze. Maybe I was pushing too far, but I needed a change of subject. I needed to know something of worth because the guilt was already crawling across my skin. And a voice at the back of my mind was asking again and again, What have you done?

She said, "I don't know what you're talking about."

She looked away, but I used a finger on her jaw to bring her eyes back to mine. "It's just . . . I look at you, and I see a beautiful woman in the prime of her life, traveling to exotic places, with the world at her fingertips. But I think that's just what you want people to see. And maybe I love a mystery too, because I can't seem to make myself stop thinking about what's underneath all that, what you *don't* let people see."

I brought my other hand up, cradling her face. Concentrating on her instead of the monumental mistake I'd just made, instead of everything I'd just thrown away.

It didn't work. She pushed my hands off and pulled out of my reach.

"I told you . . . I don't know what you're talking about. I was wasted. You shouldn't take one person's drunk ramblings as truth."

She turned away, picked up my abandoned drink, and gulped half of it down in one pull. I was relieved. If she drank that, one less thing to tempt me.

"I don't believe you," I said. "I think it was the most honest thing you've said to me. Maybe to yourself, too."

She stayed facing away from me as she said, "Again with the knight-in-shining armor bullshit. I don't need you to take care of me. You don't know anything about me. So whatever you think you're doing, whatever you're trying to *fix* in me, you can fuck off."

She took another big gulp, and I noticed her hands were shaking. All week, I'd been thinking about whether or not she was going to crash again, and now I might be the one pushing her to it.

"Hey, I'm sorry. Don't be upset."

I stood behind her, my hands hovering above her shoulders.

"I'm not upset."

She threw back the rest of the drink, and then slammed it down on the bar. Immediately, she raised her hand to try to get the bartender's attention.

I stopped hesitating and grabbed her hand. I pressed it down against the bar and leaned my lips down to her ear. Softly, I said, "Kelsey, I'm sorry. I shouldn't have pushed. But don't drink because you're mad at me."

Don't drink because *I'm* mad at me and took it out on you.

I'd already fucked-up enough tonight for the both of us.

She turned her head toward me, but kept her eyes on the bartender.

"Apology accepted. And I'm drinking because I *want* to."

"Just talk to me for a second."

She ignored me, raising her other hand and calling out.

I spun her around by her elbow and trapped her between my arms and the bar. My guilt fizzled as the feel of her body against mine took precedence in my head.

"What the hell is your problem?"

"I just needed to talk to you for a second."

"So you manhandle me like a caveman? Jesus!"

This was going so completely wrong. All because I touched that damn drink. I smiled, willing her to understand that I didn't mean any harm.

"I just wanted to apologize."

"You already did that."

"I know. But I really am sorry."

So goddamn sorry.

"I don't think you are. There's this pattern that keeps

cropping up, where you judge me when you have no right to do so. And when you're not judging me, you're prying into my life."

"I'm not judging you. I promise. And the rest? That's just the soldier in me . . . I'm too straightforward. If I want to know something, I just ask. If I want to do something, I do it."

Even when it is really, *really* stupid.

"Yeah, subtlety is definitely not your strong suit."

I smiled, because she wasn't struggling against me anymore. "No. It definitely isn't."

Neither, apparently, was control. She'd been fascinating from afar, but having met her, I decided *consuming* was the better word.

"Well, then. If you'll let me go, I think I'm going to go find Jenny and the others. Since I'm not *allowed* to order another drink and—"

I'd already indulged one desire tonight, about which I would feel immensely guilty in the morning. Why not make it two?

I lifted my hands up from the bar to grasp her jaw. Then I set out to discover exactly what her lips tasted like.

12

SHE HESITATED WHEN my lips touched hers, but not for long. I traced my tongue across her bottom lip in the same way her tongue had on more than one occasion, and she opened to me immediately. She tasted sweet, just like I thought she would. And despite what I thought, I couldn't taste a drop of alcohol, only her.

Her fingernails dug into the back of my neck, and I was hard almost instantly. I groaned against her lips as they pressed harder, faster against my own. I reached for her waist, but her swimsuit was in the way of my fingertips finding skin. I slipped one hand around to her back, pressing it flat against her smooth skin. She arched her back, crushing her chest against mine, and I wanted to devour her.

I pulled her bottom lip between my teeth just for a second, and her hands pressed down on my shoulders. Then I set about tasting the rest of her. The corner of her lips, her jaw, the long column of her neck. I leaned her back into the bar, my hips snug against hers so that there was no way she didn't know exactly how much I wanted her.

She pulled my face up to hers and said, "I think I like your lack of subtlety."

My only reply was to kiss her again. To have more of her. My newest addiction. I didn't know how long we kissed except that my lips were raw, and it was still not *enough*. I could have spent another day, maybe two, just exploring her mouth.

She was the one to pull back, breathing heavy.

"Wow."

I leaned my forehead against hers and said, "I should have just done that from the start."

Her eyes fluttered closed, and she leaned harder into me, but didn't say anything.

"Don't tell me you're speechless, princess."

A tiny, tinkling laugh bubbled up from her mouth, and it was unlike any other noise I'd heard her make. She looked shocked, and let go of me to cover her mouth.

As I smiled at her, she started slumping sideways.

"Whoa!" I wrapped my arms around her waist, and her head thumped against my chest. She turned her face, pressing her cheek against my skin.

"Kelsey?" What the hell was going on?

She didn't answer, but she was leaning almost all her weight on me now.

"My cheeks," she mumbled.

"What about them, princess?"

She turned her head so that her forehead pressed against my chest again, her lips touching my skin. My heart raced in its cage. She made a noise, small and soft and pathetic almost. Unease curled in my gut.

I kept one arm around her waist, and used the other to pull her head up to mine. "Kelsey? What were you saying about your cheeks?"

"Can't feel."

"You can't feel your cheeks?"

She didn't reply, but when I loosened my grip on her jaw, her head began to fall immediately.

"Shit."

Something wasn't right.

I tilted her head back again, searching her eyes. Wide pupils, unfocused gaze. One of the neon lights overhead swept over us, and she winced, pulling away. The minute she was out of my arms, she collapsed. I narrowly managed to catch her before she hit the ground.

I tried to get her to look at me, but her eyes kept wandering.

"Kelsey, you didn't have anything to drink earlier, did you?"

She opened her mouth but paused . . . for one, two, three seconds. When I was about to ask her again, she shook her head.

"Damn it. My drink."

That was the only explanation. I'd set it on the bar, and it had been there unattended for . . . I didn't know . . . a few minutes at least.

I held her tight between my body and the bar and snapped my fingers for the bartender's attention. "This drink." I held up the empty glass. "Did you see anyone mess with it? Anyone touch it besides me or her?"

The guy shrugged, and then went back to take someone else's order.

Goddamn it.

I let go of Kelsey's waist to scrape my fingers across my scalp. She started slipping, and I rushed to hold her tight against me again. I pressed my forehead against hers, trying to get her to meet my gaze.

"Everything is going to be okay, Kelsey. I'll take care of everything. I'm taking you home."

She sighed, almost sleepily, and then planted another kiss on the center of my chest before sagging against me.

She laid a hand over my heart, and if I thought I felt guilty over that drink, I was choking on it now.

"I'm sorry," I told her. "This is my fault. I should have been watching."

She lifted her head, but her eyelids were heavy, and each time she blinked, they stayed closed a little longer. She wrapped her arms around my neck, and I swept an arm underneath her legs.

With her cradled against my chest, I headed for the exit.

"I've got you, princess. You're safe. If you can hear me, no one's going to take advantage of you. I promise."

She mumbled, "Bummer."

I tried to laugh, but there was a crushing weigh on my chest, so it came out as nothing more than a breath. "You're something else."

People looked at us strangely as I waited in line to get Kelsey's things from the coat check, but no one said anything. I kept asking her questions, trying to keep her awake.

I was completely naïve of what to do in this kind of situation.

But eventually, she stopped replying, and by the time I hailed a cab outside, she was asleep.

I told the driver the address of my hotel, and once I had Kelsey lying on the backseat with her head in my lap, I rummaged through our things for the dress she'd worn a dress over her swimsuit earlier in the evening, but I didn't want to wake her to try to put it on. I laid it over the top of her so that, maybe, the taxi driver would stop staring at her through his rearview mirror. Because if he didn't, his face was going to get to know that mirror really well.

I tried to swallow down the guilt cloying at the back of my throat, but it didn't budge. I brushed Kelsey's hair out of her face, letting my knuckles graze the curve of her cheek.

She was so beautiful. And it tore me to pieces to see her this vulnerable.

Because if she was anything like me, and I believed she was, it must kill her to be weak. It had taken me so long to deal with losing Rodriguez and Johnny and Teague and Ingram. For a time, it had been easier to cut them out completely, to burn out those memories with bitterness and distractions, so that no one had to see how completely dismantled I was.

I felt that same way now . . . . dismantled. Like all I wanted to do was to hold Kelsey and piece her together, but I too was just a mess of parts, incapable of helping her in the way I wanted.

Maybe I couldn't save her. People can only save themselves.

But I could be there for her like Rodriguez had been for me. I could take the bottle or her pain or her past or whatever it was that made her *tired* and use it for target practice just like Rodriguez had done for me. And maybe if we were lucky, our demons would be the dismantled ones.

When we were almost to the hotel, the driver took a turn too fast, and I had to hold her waist and shoulder to keep her from tumbling onto the floorboard.

She stirred. "What's happening?"

Her eyes met mine, and I felt the shift in my thinking take root. I couldn't leave her. Wouldn't.

"We're in a cab. I can't be certain, but . . ." I tried to appear calm for her sake. "I'm pretty sure someone slipped something in that drink while it was sitting on the bar."

She laid a hand across her eyes and groaned, "Fuck."

"I tell you that you've been roofied and that's all you have to say?"

"You tell me I've been roofied and expect me to say *more*?"

Even drugged, she had an attitude. And even though I wanted to get mad, I couldn't. Not when she was like this. I trailed my fingers through her damp hair, wishing I could do more.

She laid a hand over mine on her stomach, lacing our fingers together. She fell asleep that way, but we arrived at the hotel less than a minute later.

I paid the driver, and then as carefully as I could, maneuvered her out of the cab. I tried my best to keep her covered by her dress, but the desk clerk still stared as I entered the building.

I didn't bother getting her a new room. There wasn't enough time, and I didn't want her out in public like this any longer than she had to be.

She blinked up at me in the elevator, her lips marred by a frown.

"You scare me," she said.

The air turned solid in my lungs. What did she think I would do to her? I struggled to take a deeper breath and then, as slowly and calmly as I could, said, "You have nothing to be scared of. I won't . . . I wouldn't. I'll help you get to bed, and then I'll leave, get another room."

She shook her head.

"Not that. I don't think that."

"Then why do I scare you?"

"Because I don't want you to see."

She wasn't making any sense. She didn't want me to see her like this? The situation was hardly her fault, and it wasn't as though I hadn't been there the other night when she'd been so drunk that she'd gotten sick.

"See what?"

I shouldered open the door to my hotel room at the same time that she said, "Me."

I stood in the entryway for a few moments, stunned into silence before I felt the cold, wet fabric of her swimsuit soaking through my T-shirt. I crossed the room quickly and gently lowered her into a cushioned chair.

I laid the things I'd gotten from the coat check at her feet, and then knelt in front of her.

"Why wouldn't you want me to see you, Kelsey?"

She sealed her lips and shook her head.

"Kelsey, look at me."

She did, reluctantly. She looked miserable. I pushed a lock of hair behind her ear. It was selfish, but I wanted to be the one person who got to *see* her. I wanted to be the only one with whom she didn't feel the need to hide. "You are beautiful, that's all I see."

Her eyes went glassy, and I hated not knowing what to do to help her. As I watched, her head began to nod and she struggled to stay upright.

I cleared my throat, but still didn't know what to do. She needed to rest. That was my best guess. "I, um, we should get you out of your wet swimsuit."

I felt sick thinking about it, but I also didn't want her to get a cold from sleeping in wet clothes.

She yawned. "Okay." She tried to stand, but her legs wobbled and she started sinking back toward the chair before I caught her. She looked up at me as our bodies pressed together, and I had to force my eyes away because I swear I saw desire there.

She fumbled with the knot at her hip, where her complicated swimsuit connected. I watched her uselessly pluck at the fabric, her fingers weak.

In a small, quiet voice, she said, "I can't."

I had hold of her arms, but the rest of her body began to fall.

"It's okay. I'll help. It's okay."

Anything to take that crushed look off her face.

I lowered her into the chair, but then took a few steps back because, fuck, I needed some distance. I exhaled, dragging my hands across the top of my head and down over my face.

"What the fuck am I doing?"

How in the world was I supposed to do this?

God, give me combat. Give me death and destruction. But this? I didn't know how to deal with *this*.

"Okay," I said aloud. I could do it. Quick. Efficient. Just enough to make her comfortable. "Okay."

Decided, I went to my suitcase and grabbed a clean T-shirt before returning to Kelsey. I got down on my knees in front of her and met her eyes. "Here, slip this on."

This way I couldn't see anything. Wouldn't see anything.

She nodded, but didn't move. After slipping the shirt over her head, I had to maneuver her arms through the sleeves. I was almost done when my forearm brushed against her chest, and she made a soft, sweet noise.

Fuck. Sorry. Damn it.

I berated myself silently before saying quietly, "Sorry." Then I finished pulling the shirt on as fast as I could. Her eyes were more alert, and she watched my every move with a hunger in her gaze that was going to make this so much harder. I lowered her arm to her side, and then retreated to the other side of the room for another short break.

"Okay. Next step," I said aloud, trying to approach this tactically. I needed to untie the knots at her hips, and then unwind the straps of fabric that wrapped around her waist and chest before attaching to the thin straps over her shoulders.

I lifted her from the chair and, with her in my arms, dragged back the covers on the bed. I laid her down and pulled the covers up to cover her.

I considered stopping there. But she shivered, and I knew I couldn't.

I turned on the lamp next to the bed and knelt beside her. Then, like I was undressing my eighty-six-year-old grandma instead of Kelsey, I reached under the covers and found the knot of the swimsuit at her hip.

She stared at me, and I could only smile in a way that I hoped wasn't creepy.

"Are you that scared of seeing me naked?" she asked.

I finished with the first knot quickly, detaching the strap of her top from her bottoms.

"I'm not scared, sweetheart." In fact, I liked the idea entirely too much for me to feel comfortable in this situation. I added, "I promise I won't look."

I stretched my arm farther under the covers, trying to uncoil the fabric from her waist, but the rest of it wound beneath her body and I couldn't manage to slide it out.

"Can you lift yourself up? That might be easier. "

She tried. She tried so hard.

"I can't." Her voice shook, and I wanted to pour out a thousand apologies for making her feel weak.

I stood and sat on the bed next to her.

"Wrap your arms around my neck, and use me to pull yourself up."

Slowly, she pulled her arms out from under the covers. I had to help her wrap her hands around the back of my neck, though.

"Just hold on."

With her sitting up, I slipped my hands beneath the hem of the T-shirt that bunched around her hips. I pulled on the strap I'd untied from her hip, expecting it to unwind around her back to her chest. But when I pulled, nothing happened. The other part of the wrap must have been in the way.

"Damn it. The other piece is strapped over this one. Hang on."

I snuck another hand beneath the T-shirt and under the material of her swimsuit. Holding the still taut piece of fabric out from her skin, I started pulling on the other strap. Kelsey's fingers dug into the back of my neck, reminiscent of the way they had when we kissed, and I had to pause to keep control. It didn't help that her breath was skating across my jaw, warm and maddening.

"Hunt?"

I swallowed.

"Yeah?"

As I pulled the fabric from the first strap free, her fingers trailed from my neck to my jaw. "Tell me your other name. The one most people don't call you."

I paused to look in her eyes. Better than looking at her lips.

"You won't remember it tomorrow, sweetheart."

"Doesn't mean I don't want to know, *sweetheart*."

So much attitude.

I smiled briefly. With one strap loose, I let the hand that was holding the rest of the fabric up rest against her back. She swallowed, glancing down at my lips.

"Jackson. My name is Jackson Hunt."

She smiled, and I returned it because I couldn't help it.

"Well, Jackson Hunt. Stop being a pansy, and just take my clothes off."

I laughed. Because this whole damn situation was ridiculous.

"You're something else, you know that?"

"Like you said, I won't remember it tomorrow. Let's just get it over with."

I groaned, scratching my nails across my jaw.

"But I'll remember." And I would never be able to look at her the same again.

She sighed, and then sat back against the pillow. My hand shifted from her back to her side as she lay down. With shaky hands, she pushed the covers down to her thighs, revealing the T-shirt that was bunched up around her rib cage.

I tore my hand away from where it curled around her waist and looked away from her smooth golden skin.

"Jesus, Kelsey."

"It's not that big of a deal."

"It is, though. I can't take advantage of you like that. Not when you're not sober enough to make decisions with a clear head."

She groaned. "You're not taking advantage of me. Been there. Done that. It felt nothing like this."

I jerked my head around.

"What did you say?"

"Nothing."

That hadn't sounded like nothing.

"Kelsey—"

Who had taken advantage of her? Suddenly, I was so angry that I couldn't see straight. All the pieces of me that had felt broken and useless where suddenly fused together, ready to fight whatever enemy had hurt her.

"It doesn't matter," she said. "Just help me. Please? *Please.*"

I wanted to push her, but pushing was what had gotten us in this mess to begin with. If I'd never had that drink, never asked her that question . . .

I thought back to that moment in the elevator when her emerald eyes had met mine, and she said I scared her. I took a deep breath and tried to think like Rodriguez. He'd never pushed me to talk about my issues, not about the mom who left or the dad who didn't care. He waited until I opened up on my own.

After a sigh, I did as she asked. With the covers back and the T-shirt up, I untied the other knot. I told myself it wasn't any more than I'd seen at the baths. But when I began unwrapping the rest of the swimsuit from her body, I made sure my eyes were directed at her face. I was not going to be added to the list of people who'd taken advantage of her, who'd hurt her.

I leaned down over her and used a hand to lift up her midsection so I could unwrap the last strap. Too eager to be finished, I yanked on the swimsuit top and it slid off her body completely.

She gasped, arching her back, and her stomach brushed against my chest. I made a noise of frustration and exasperation, and slammed my eyes closed before I could be tempted to look.

As quickly as possible, I pulled the suit free from her arms and tossed it on the floor. I was still leaning over her when I opened my eyes. I looked at her lips, just for a second. But then she whimpered and . . . *Damn it.*

She breathed, "Jackson."

She closed her eyes and lifted her lips toward mine. I knew she was attracted to me. And I'd thrown all my morals out the window when I kissed her earlier tonight, but I couldn't do it again.

No matter how much I wanted to.

I owed her more than that.

I shifted away from her lips and kissed her cheek instead.

"I can't. Not like this. If I'm going to cross this line, I sure as hell want you to remember it."

Her hands gripped my waist.

"It's not crossing a line if I want it."

I swear to God she was like a siren. That's why no one could say no to her.

"I want you, too. But you have no idea how many lines I'd be crossing, even if you were sober."

"What does that mean?"

"It means I'm getting you ready for bed, and then I'm saying good night."

"Then get me ready for bed."

She took my hand and placed it on her hip, where her swimsuit bottoms still rested. Needing to be done with this, I hooked my fingers under the fabric and pulled. I kept my eyes on the ceiling as I slipped the bottoms down her legs and past her feet. Then I pulled the blankets all the way up to her chin.

She caught my hand before I could pull away, holding it close to her face. My heart lurched.

"Don't go."

I smoothed a hand across my jaw.

"I have to. This isn't a good idea."

"I don't want to wake up alone. If I don't remember . . . I'll . . . it will kill me. You don't know . . ."

There was that mystery again. That glimpse of something that she wasn't telling me, that she didn't show anyone. That thing I couldn't *push* to untangle no matter how tempted I was.

"Jackson, please."

I couldn't say no to her.

"Okay. Just . . . just give me a second."

In the bathroom, I shucked off my own wet swim trunks in favor of some gym shorts. I looked in the mirror, but then wished I hadn't.

I looked rough.

Maybe it was the lack of sleep. Maybe it was that tonight I'd undone a year of hard work and commitment.

Either way, I was more worried about Kelsey than I was about me.

I would survive. That was what I did . . . against all odds. And somehow I knew that I wouldn't relapse after that one drink, not when it could impair my ability to take care of *her*.

There was a sickening, sinking feeling in my gut that unraveled into theories about Kelsey and her past, and I wanted to punch something just so I didn't have to think about it anymore.

Whatever had happened to her, there was more to Kelsey Summer's story. There was a reason my drawings of her only worked when she looked sad.

Back in the room, I turned off the lamp beside the bed and settled down in the chair to sleep for the night.

I didn't know Kelsey Summers. But I wanted to. If she would open up, if she would let me. I was a little afraid to admit how much I wanted from her.

Ten minutes after Kelsey fell asleep, my phone buzzed. Kelsey's father.

No matter what I wanted, I was the last person in the world she should trust.

COMING SOON FROM
CORA CARMACK

**Texas, college football, and
heart-stopping romance.
The perfect recipe for an unforgettable
news series you won't want to miss from
New York Times and *USA Today*
bestselling author Cora Carmack.**

ALL LINED UP
Rusk University, BOOK 1

*Two things in Texas are cherished above all else—
football and gossip.
My life has always been ruled by both.*

When your dad is a coaching legend in Texas high school
football, your life isn't your own. Which is why Dallas
Cole can't wait to get to Rusk University and finally get
out of her father's shadow. But when he makes the jump

to college ball—at her school, no less—it's déjà vu all over again.

Half the guys on campus avoid her like the plague—not wanting to come close to the notorious hard-ass coach's daughter—and the other half want to use her to get closer to the legend.

And then there's Carson McClain, the hot, newly transferred second-string quarterback. *He* has no idea who she is, so when Carson approaches her at a party, Dallas decides, for once in her life, to kiss first and ask questions later. . . .

Coming Spring 2014

And don't miss any of Cora Carmack's
New York Times **and** ***USA Today*** **bestselling**

LOSING IT SERIES

Available Now

LOSING IT
Book 1

Virginity.

Bliss Edwards is about to graduate from college and still has hers. Sick of being the only virgin among her friends, she decides the best way to deal with the problem is to lose it as quickly and simply as possible—a one-night stand. But her plan turns out to be anything but simple when she freaks out and leaves a gorgeous guy alone and naked in her bed with an excuse that no one with half a brain would ever believe.

And as if that weren't embarrassing enough, when she arrives for her first class of her last college semester, she recognizes her new theater professor.

She'd left him naked in her bed about eight hours earlier.

KEEPING HER
A *Losing It* Novella

Garrick Taylor and Bliss Edwards managed to find their happily-ever-after despite a rather . . . ahem . . . complicated start. By comparison, meeting the parents should be an absolute breeze, right?

But from the moment the pair lands in London, new snags just keep cropping up: a disapproving mother-in-law to be, an ex-girlfriend bent on a reunion, and a role in a play that will lead to nothing but trouble.

Garrick never imagined that the only thing harder than finding love is keeping it.

FAKING IT
Book 2

Mackenzie "Max" Miller has a problem. Her parents have arrived in town for a surprise visit, and if they see her dyed hair, tattoos, and piercings, they just might disown her. Even worse, they're expecting to meet a nice whole-some boyfriend, not a guy named Mace who has a neck tattoo and plays in a band. All her lies are about to come crashing down around her, but then she meets Cade.

Cade moved to Philadelphia to act and to leave his problems behind in Texas. So far, though, he's kept the problems and had very little opportunity to take the stage. When Max approaches him in a coffee shop with a crazy request to pretend to be her boyfriend, he agrees to play the part. But when Cade plays the role a little too well, they're forced to keep the ruse going. And the more they fake the relationship, the more real it begins to feel.

FINDING IT
Book 3

Most girls would kill to spend months traveling around Europe after college graduation with no responsibility, no parents, and no-limit credit cards. Kelsey Summers is no exception. She's having the time of her life . . . or that's what she keeps telling herself.

It's a lonely business trying to find out who you are, especially when you're afraid you won't like what you discover. No amount of drinking or dancing can chase away Kelsey's loneliness, but maybe Jackson Hunt can. After a few chance meetings, he convinces her to take a journey of adventure instead of alcohol. With each new city and experience, Kelsey's mind becomes a little clearer and her heart a little less hers. Jackson helps her unravel her own dreams and desires. But the more she learns about herself, the more Kelsey realizes how little she knows about Jackson.

SEEKING HER
A *Finding It* Prequel

Jackson Hunt hasn't been out of the military for a long, but he needs to get a job and find a sense of normalcy if he is going to keep his own demons at bay. The job that falls into his lap, though, is anything but normal.

Bodyguard (and babysitter) to spoiled-rich-girl Kelsey Summers isn't exactly what he'd been looking for, but it's a chance to travel, to get away. The catch: Kelsey's father doesn't want Kelsey to know she's being followed.

She's vibrant and infuriating, exciting and reckless, mysterious and familiar. When Jackson sees her falling into the same patterns he suffered years ago, he decides it's time to stop watching and help her instead. But getting to know Kelsey is more difficult than he thought, especially because the more he knows her, the more he wants her.

ABOUT THE AUTHOR

CORA CARMACK is a twenty-something writer who likes to write about twenty-something characters. She's done a multitude of things in her life—retail, theatre, teaching, and writing. She loves theatre, travel, and anything that makes her laugh. She enjoys placing her characters in the most awkward situations possible, and then trying to help them get a boyfriend out of it. Awkward people need love, too.

Visit www.AuthorTracker.com for exclusive information on your favorite HarperCollins authors.

31192020628705